THE LIGHT BEHIND THE MASK

KAREN L ROSE

ISBN: 979-8-9908862-0-9 (hardcover)
ISBN: 979-8-9908862-1-6 (paperback)
ISBN: 979-8-9908862-2-3 (ebook)

To my dad, Seymour, and my two moms Fay and Beatrice, for always giving me support, love, and guidance.

ACKNOWLEDGEMENTS

Please Hear What I'm Not Saying with permission from Charles C. Finn, author.

CHAPTER 1

Mattie Newport was excited. She was going on a date, finally, and even though her mother refused to acknowledge that her daughter was old enough to leave the house with a boy, Delores dropped her head onto her chest with an audible sigh when Mattie raced into the kitchen.

"Look, Ma!" Mattie exclaimed with such fierce energy, "Look at what I'm wearing tonight! I borrowed this from Roslyn. It doesn't fit her anymore and she said I could keep it! Isn't it the bomb? I mean, sorry, Ma, I mean isn't this the prettiest dress you have ever seen in your whole life?"

Delores lifted her head slowly and scrutinized her daughter deliberately, carefully, as though she were seeing her for the first time. Mattie had grown into a beautiful woman at eighteen with her high cheekbones, crystal blue eyes, and auburn hair; Delores knew she was a fine-looking young woman. And this is what caused her such anguish. *I never wanted you to be this pretty. Being pretty comes with a lot of responsibility. Boys are always wanting to do that thing with you. You must always be on your guard. You must watch your step wherever you go. Even those seemingly inno-cent neighbors, they are animals, every single one of them. I know. I know. I know because…*

Delores pushed her sigh out slowly. She couldn't go there. It wasn't fair. Not today anyway. And besides, that was a long time ago. The hairs on the back of her neck curled up with the memory of his one large hand gripping her small neck and his other rough hand groping her, telling her all the while she was beautiful, that he wanted her, needed her, and it was okay because no one would ever know that he was defiling her. Delores had pushed this awful and disgusting memory down so deep inside her she refused to say his name. He was her mother's best friend's son; he was their neighbor, and everyone adored him. How could Delores ever tell her mother that when he offered to help her with her complicated homework, he was doing things to her that made her stomach churn. She was filled with shame, and she could not tell anyone, not ever.

But her daughter didn't deserve to know any of that old baggage. Delores reached for another cigarette, her last one in the pack, and lit it carefully, taking a long drag and letting the soft white billowy cloud slide gently from her lips. She stared at the pale-yellow peeling paint in her kitchen; she ignored the slow drip, drip from the sink faucet. Her eyes glazed over as she followed the dissipating smoke up to the ceiling.

"Yeah, honey, you look like a movie star. You could be a

model one day, ya know if you play your cards right. Hey, let me do your hair up real nice for ya. I know all the latest styles. I seen 'em at the salon all the time."

"No, Ma…it's okay," answered Mattie. "I like my hair down like this. Listen, I gotta go now. Please stop smoking, Ma…you know it's not good for you. The doctor told you to stop, remember? Okay, now make sure you eat some dinner, okay? I left the spaghetti from the other night all wrapped up for you, so you just need to reheat it on the stove, okay?"

Delores watched her only daughter race out of the kitchen with such positive energy and hope for all her tomorrows. Delores knew deep down, so deep she did not want to let it surface, but she knew that Mattie was not always going to be this happy, this exuberant. It wasn't meant to be; it wasn't in her cards. A few tears slipped onto her puffy cheeks as she crushed the empty cigarette pack and looked desperately around the aged and dilapidated kitchen for a new one.

Mattie let the screen door slam as she raced out of her house breathing in a new sensation: freedom. *This is what I have been waiting for all my life!* Mattie gazed up at the setting sun, the soft cool breezes of autumn gently caressing her face. She smiled to herself. Mattie was so excited she could barely control her emotions and she was not going to let her mother bring her down, not tonight anyway.

Mattie stood at the edge of the curb waiting. He was supposed to pick her up thirty minutes ago. The exuberance she had felt only a little while ago seemed to have melted along with the foundation on her face she had put on so carefully. She kept staring down the street, hoping that the next car would be his, playing games in her head – *okay I'll count to 20 and then he will be here. Okay, I'll count to thirty and then….* This game seemed to go on forever and Mattie squeezed her eyes tight almost willing the next car to be the magical one.

And so she waited….and waited….and waited.

Finally, when the sun had long kissed the top of the trees goodnight and the stars twinkled their hello's, Mattie turned and slowly, as though walking to her execution, sluggishly trudged back into her home, turning on the living room lights as she entered, knowing her mom was already finished with her nightly drinking and her cigarettes and would be up in her bedroom watching some old movie.

Mattie looked around the living room as if she were seeing it for the first time. The old, worn plaid couch that her mom had lovingly patched up on the arm rests, the large orange chair (ugh, what an ugly color for a chair) that had bite marks on the legs from their mutt who ran away last year never to be found, and the coffee table riddled with water marks from too many drinks left behind in a drunken state never to be cleaned up till morning.

"I live in a dump," said Mattie with tears in her soft sky-blue eyes and her throat tight from crying the entire last hour. "I live in a dump," she repeated to herself, "so who would want to date me anyways?" Mattie sighed, and dejected with everything around her, plodded into the kitchen and sat down at the stained linoleum table.

Mattie stared at the glass cigarette tray overflowing with ashes and red lipstick-stained half-smoked butts. Her mother's glass sat in a pool of liquid from the condensation gliding down the glass. Mattie's brain was reeling, and her thoughts were all over the place from why doesn't my mother care about her drinking and smoking to why didn't boys like her to where is she going to live when she graduated high school to what is she going to do with the rest of her life.

Rather than stick to any one of those deep thoughts, Mattie picked up one of the longer butts from the tray, snatched the book of matches that lay open next to the glass, and lit the cigarette. Mattie took one long drag and inhaled the smoke the way she saw her mother do it. The smoke slid down her throat irritating her tonsils so that she coughed uncontrollably. She reached for the glass, glared at it as if daring the amber liquid to deny her a drink, and before she could talk herself out of it, put the rim to her lips and slugged it down quickly. The burning sensation eased the coughing, and the fire in her throat was a welcome feeling.

Mattie took another puff of what was left of the cigarette and this time she did not swallow the smoke; instead, she gently blew it out of her mouth the way she had watched her favorite actress perform it at the movies. She took another sip of the alcohol controlling the smooth liquid so that it rolled over her tongue and slid down her throat treasuring the fluid as though it was pure gold.

Mattie leaned back, took another drag of the cigarette, and smiled. She felt like a pro after a few hits and savored the way her body discovered a new tranquility of its own. After a few more sips of the leftover scotch, Mattie's body reached a drunken euphoria.

I could get used to this sensation, she thought. *Feel no pain. Feel no want. Feel no sadness.*

And so it began.

CHAPTER 2

Winter break was just around the corner and Neva Waverly was worried, and she was not a worrier. The cuticles on her fingers had scabs from where she had been chewing on them until they bled. She had not spoken to Carl in over two months; no one had. No one was allowed to contact Carl since he was escorted out of the building and there was not a single staff member who had any answers. Their faces were oddly blank today, hiding any emotion regarding Carl and it saddened Neva because he was their colleague, their friend. Neva had brought up Carl's absence during their last team meeting, and watching her teammates scrunch up their foreheads, shake their heads, and roll their eyes only increased her anxiety.

Neva stared at her notebook, forcing herself not to show any tears. She did not want to appear weak or too emotionally involved, but where was their loyalty? The team had morphed from shock and dismay and anger to pathetic silence or was it total indifference?

"I have no clue," stated Sam Tannereck coldly, "but it does seem awfully weird that he is not here, and no one knows why."

Alisa Saper glanced at Beverly Winewrought. Beverly kept her eyes on the paper in front of her, letting her long fingers comb through her short black hair, and shrugged her shoulders. Suddenly she looked up and said with venom dripping in her tone, "Well, if you ask me, he got what he deserved. Afterall, no one is suddenly scooped out of a building and not heard from again. This isn't the time of the mafia or street gangs who kidnap people in broad daylight never to be seen again. And besides, the damn cops were here for Christ's sake. Can we get on with the agenda now?" Beverly glared at everyone around the table long enough to fill the air with so much tension everyone seemed to droop under the weight of it.

Barbara Atkinson sat massaging her chin. She kept pulling at a few stray gray hairs that refused to depart her dimpled soft skin. She was studying Beverly closely trying to cram into her head what Beverly was really thinking, but afraid to know the truth because Barbara truly believed Beverly's soul was dark and evil.

The team room was silent. The long rectangular table was littered with composition books, folders, used coffee cups, pens, and pencils of all kinds, and a paper plate half filled with stale Danishes. Raizel Glenstone suddenly pushed her chair back and got up. She went over to the window and opened it and let the cool winter air fill her lungs. She needed to share some information and she wasn't quite sure how to begin. She returned to her chair and slumped into it; she was tired.

Neva observed Raizel. Raizel, with her frizzy auburn hair tied in a huge bun on top of her head, had been teaching physical education for over fifteen years now and she had tremendous insight into her students. When kids have to change their clothes in a large locker room, perform physically in groups – especially when they are not athletically proficient – or discuss very private, serious issues during health classes, Raizel sees a completely different and often times vulnerable side to her students.

"Look, I know we are all concerned about Carl. None of us have heard from him, have we?" Raizel looked around the room. Everyone looked at Raizel, nodding in agreement. Everyone, that is, except Beverly. Beverly was once again staring at a pile of papers in front of her.

No one said a word. They didn't have to. Everyone in the room knew how close Neva and Carl were. Are. They taught their mentoring program side by side for months until, well, until the incident.

"Neva?" Raizel asked. "Neva, have you spoken with Carl?"

Neva lifted her chin and looked at each of her colleagues one at a time, skipping past Beverly who still had her beady eyes focused on her papers, and then stopping with Barbara. Neva took a slow, deep breath and said defiantly, "I am not allowed to speak with Carl. No one is. And, therefore, if I had spoken to him, well, that would be illegal, and sharing that information with you would put all of you, and Carl for that matter, at risk. So. To be sure today I have not spoken to Carl. Enough said. Let's move this meeting on because we only have a few more minutes until the period ends and I have to update my computer's opening drill before the kids come rushing in."

Barbara caught the implication. *Today*, Neva had said. She had not spoken with Carl *today*. That clearly meant that she had been in contact with Carl. But Barbara was in no position of authority to judge Neva, let alone reprimand her. This case was out of her hands, and she was not going to interfere. And she hoped everyone at the table was having the same thoughts. That is until she focused again on Beverly. Beverly's tightly pressed lips and her squinting dark brown eyes exhibited such an intense level of hatred that only Barbara was privy to since Beverly had stormed into her office that day and screamed and ranted about not getting the mentoring position.

"Okay, group, let's get back on track. We have a substitute for Carl, and I will be asking him to join us tomorrow. And, no, he has not spoken with Carl either. But I would appreciate your professionalism when he joins us and not give him the third degree, okay?"

Neva continued, Barbara took notes, Beverly stared out the window and the rest of the team kept their focus on Neva.

"We have been working with these students for most of the first semester and I want to go over our flag list. We will need to explain to Alex, Carl's sub, what we mean by our flag list. Remember, we are not targeting students, just flagging those we worry about for either academic, emotional, physical, or other reasons. This doesn't mean that if a student is not currently on our flag list, he or she can't be added to it, but more importantly, once a student is on our list then we do not remove that student; the student can be shifted to the bottom of the list, but always remains. Understood?"

The team nodded in unison. They all knew that Neva was doing her job and not being condescending or patronizing. She was given the respect she deserved. Only Beverly refused to acknowledge Neva's leadership role. She nodded but never made eye contact. This was her way of demonstrating that while she was on the team and agreed with everyone, she was not really a part of them.

"Okay," continued Neva, "Alisa, since this is your first year on the team with us, and yes, I know you are an awesome veteran teacher, I want you to start us off by being in charge of identifying the students on the list. Once you read a name, then, team, let's see where we are and where we can do the most good."

Alisa felt empowered by Neva. She fully regarded Neva as a tremendous and positive leader even though Beverly was always bashing her outside of the team meetings. Alisa may have been good friends with Beverly, but she wasn't completely swayed by her bias. Beverly had her own demons to deal with and Alisa did not appreciate being pulled in to join her doom and gloom mentality.

"Mmmm, excuse me," began Alisa. She was nervous as she flipped her long black box braids onto her back. Her deep coffee bean brown eyes flittered around the table and her soft mahogany-toned hands shook just enough to show she was nervous about this role. She smiled, a million-dollar smile that lit up the room and then she started slowly and clearly, "Well, it looks like we have eight students right now who are part of our at-risk group. There have been changes in the order of their level of urgency, most notably Cindy Newport. Cindy was our number one at-risk student in September, but as of now, she has moved to the bottom of our rankings. Between seeing her therapist weekly and attending the mentoring program after school along with consistent communications with her mom, Cindy has been flourishing."

Alisa took a deep breath and looked at Neva for approval. Neva smiled, her eyes twinkling, and she nodded, encouraging Alisa to continue.

With each student, Alisa's confidence grew, and she was able to read each write-up carefully and authoritatively. Today was not the day to go into great depth about each student; today was an overview of the list prior to the end of the first semester. It was time to review, revise, and revisit each student.

"Before we conclude today," Alisa said, sounding a bit exhausted at this point, "we do have one new student to add to the list. Although I have gone over all the names save one, I would like to ask Raizel to talk about our new addition. Ms. Glenstone, the floor is all yours as they say."

Raizel Glenstone, her short, chaotic auburn hair fell carelessly in her round face and her hazel eyes twinkled in the sun rays that streaked in the window and landed on her like a spotlight.

Raizel cleared her throat and looked at each of her colleagues before she jumped in. "You know I am not usually at a loss for words, especially when it comes to our students, but I gotta tell you, I really gotta tell you I am flummoxed here. I want to bring up Shaynee Moulder. Yes, she's a great academic student, but something very odd has been happening with her in the last few weeks.

"As you might realize, I always end my health unit for the ninth graders with some very, very heavy topics. I mean, after all, we have numerous speakers who visit with my students and the kids are literally hit over the head with information regarding drugs and sex and diseases, but now at the end, well, it gets a bit, how should I say…..ultra personal. Sex is always a hot topic, no pun intended here, but we have gone down an entirely new rabbit hole – genealogy."

Beverly interrupted, her boredom dripping off her face like melting wax, "So, really, Raizel, can you, uh, just get to the point? I mean, like we have been listening to you whine about your non-essential course for, duh, it seems like forever and…"

The team door suddenly thrust open with a whoosh, and Principal Lila Libertino burst into the room. She stood there in her two-inch navy heels, long, blue-flowered dress, multiple silver bracelets dangling at her wrists and her hair pulled up tight in a bun. Her left hand was gripping her walkie-talkie and her right hand was squeezing her cell phone. There was chatter on the walkie and her cell phone kept buzzing nonstop with emails. Together the two electronic objects made enough noise to create a cacophony of keyboard effects.

Dr. Libertino ignored all the extraneous chatter and bells and stared at Barbara.

"Excuse me, Ms. Atkinson," Lila said quickly and curtly, "But you are needed immediately in the main office. And why was your walkie shut off? Never mind, we will discuss that at a later time. Uhhh, sorry, everyone, to interrupt your team meeting." And with that, she gave one more look at Ms. Atkinson, turned around, and left as abruptly as she had exploded in.

Barbara Atkinson's cheeks flushed a deep red with embarrassment. She was used to barking commands at staff members privately as well as in public, but she was not accustomed to being chastised herself.

"Ummmm, excuse me, team," Barbara stammered, a bit uncomfortable in being on the other end of a seemingly disciplinary scolding, "but the big boss is calling, and I must depart. Oh, Beverly, would you please continue taking notes for me? I expect you to email them to me as soon as today's team meeting has concluded. Everyone? Thank you for a very informative meeting. Neva, thank you, always, for your professional organization and leadership."

Barbara scooped up her notebooks, her walkie, which had been turned off, and of course her cell phone and left the room quietly.

CHAPTER 3

Carl sat in his father's study, thinking, squeezing his eyes shut trying to imagine anything he might have done that would have caused him to be in so much trouble. Tiny motes drifted by like multicolored feathers brought to life from the streaks of light that slipped in between the blinds on the large bay windows. For a second Carl was hurled back in time when he would crawl under his father's large mahogany desk and hide there in fear of being found. Often times, his brother Chip would lie about something he said Carl had done, anything just to see Carl get punished. It was that same feeling of shame and guilt Carl felt now even though he knew he had done nothing wrong. Small beads of sweat clung to his nose and upper cheeks. He gently lifted his right hand from the gun, forced his sweaty fingers into a fist, and thumped himself on the forehead. *Think! Think! Think! Who did I hurt? Who was I inappropriate with and when? This is so wrong!*

And then his eyes flew open. Who wanted to hurt him? He knew he had done nothing that would cause him to be on leave, but there was that one person who despised him beyond belief. Beverly Winewrought! He never understood why she was always so angry with him. What had he done to her? He had no clue whatsoever. Could she have said something to someone? And what would she have said anyway? There was nothing to report, no action to describe, no behaviors to share. Carl had done nothing inappropriate. So why was he feeling so guilty?

Carl had met with his union representative, Lemont Jacobs. Lemont was a tall African American man with long, thick dreadlocks that covered his thinly arched eyebrows and fell softly into his light caramel eyes. Lemont was always rubbing his flat wide nose, a nervous habit he always had since he was a child.

He and Lemont hit it off immediately, but there was continuously this tiny thread of doubt Carl felt about Lemont. Lemont said over and over again, "Can you think of anything that you may have done that was inappropriate, Carl? Think hard, man. Surely, you can come up with something you may have said or did that maybe, like, you just put in the back of your head and said to yourself, 'Hey, let's not remember this 'cause it's just not cool' and that's what we need to address here and now."

Carl did not know how to respond to some of Lemont's questions. They were probing and difficult and Carl had never felt so vulnerable and violated at the same time.

Carl shook his head from side to side, the sweat flying off his face onto his arms. He felt dizzy and the room seemed to sway. The revolver in his lap felt heavy, burdensome, and cold and it seemed to whisper to him *pick me up, hold me close, cradle me tight!* Carl's eyes misted over, and the room seemed to pitch and tumble as if were on the Tilt A Wheel when he was only ten.

He was in his fourth-grade class. His seat was hard, and uncomfortable, digging into his cheap and very thin pants. He was watching Greg Stillwell a few seats over from him. Greg, tall and thin with sharp green eyes and thick black hair that fell into his eyes, glanced over at him. He smiled at Carl with straight white teeth that nobody else had since most of the guys wore braces. They were best buds, but Greg always had the girls fawning over him. The girls would push and shove each other just to stand next to Greg in line every time the class had to travel to the school library or rush to the lunchroom or march outside for a fire drill. And there they hovered near him sighing audibly. Some of the girls would push one another just to accidentally bump into him so they could brag they almost hugged Greg.

Greg was just that kind of kid who everyone wanted to be near because he was so charismatic, so kind and so funny. Right now, though he was making those ridiculous farting noises. Carl heard him and so did Wayne Planten who sat right next to Carl. Wayne was the teacher's pet and no matter what Wayne did, he never, not ever, got in trouble for it. And now Wayne, who heard Greg's ridiculous fake farting, started to snicker.

Carl was not a fan of Wayne and never had been. Wayne, with his large nose and skinny black glasses, always made fun of Carl and called him Jew boy even though Carl wasn't

Jewish. During a discussion in class about World War II, Carl said he thought he had relatives who were in the Holocaust and from then on Wayne always called him a dirty Jew among other derogatory comments. It was Carl is a lazy Jew and hey, Carl killed Christ! But today, Wayne's short snickers spilled out like he was a snorting pig and for some reason, Carl started laughing at Wayne. It was a silly sound and Carl couldn't help himself.

Suddenly, Mrs. Cratch zeroed in on Carl and shouted, "Get out of your seat, young man, and go to the back of the room! No one, and I mean no one laughs at Mrs. Cratch!"

Carl heard Wayne whistling softly at him in pure mockery. He felt the eyes of the rest of the class burning into his back as he got out of his seat and slowly shuffled to the other end of the room by the cubbies where all the students kept their coats, boots, and lunches. In the corner next to the cubbies was a sink. Mrs. Cratch grabbed Carl by the collar of his shirt, shoved him to the sink, and pushed his face down, almost slamming his nose into the faucet.

"Now you splash water on your face, young man, so you can wash that smirk off right now and don't stop till I tell you to! Do you hear me?"

Carl, his head bent over, tilted sideways to look at Mrs. Cratch, her face heavily wrinkled with hate, spittle dripping over her pale, dried, and cracked lips. She turned the cold water on full blast and shoved him in the back repeating her command, her tone so icy cold it seemed to magically form ice over the already rushing cold liquid.

Carl cupped his small hands in the frigid water and

splashed his face. The liquid tasted like iron and caused Carl to suddenly suck in the air in response to the freezing wet wall striking him in the face. Carl sputtered and spat out the water into the sink, looked over at Mrs. Cratch as she humphed at him, turned her back, and left the cubby corner.

Carl continued to slop the chilly water onto his numbing face for the next ten minutes. Shaking from the cold, Carl just stopped. He spat the extra water into the sink, turned off the faucet, rubbed his sleeves over his face, and turned around to see what was happening in his classroom. It was empty. Everyone had gone to lunch, leaving Carl alone in the back of the room with his punishment.

Mrs. Cratch looked up from her desk, her dull brown eyes staring at him. "Well, you evil little boy, are you thoroughly finished laughing at me?"

Carl knew better than to argue. It wasn't worth it. She wasn't worth it. He knew he wasn't going to win so he just nodded and wiped the snot rolling down his nose with the back of his hand.

"Go on, then. Get out of here. Go find our class in the lunchroom and see if anyone will sit with you because you are a worthless little nothing. Now go on. Leave."

Carl walked slowly out of the classroom; his eyes moist with tears that he fought so hard to control. She was not going to make him cry. He did nothing wrong. He was a good kid. He sniffed the rest of the snot back up his nose and left the room.

Carl shook his head from side to side physically trying to erase that old memory. Those were some of the experiences that motivated Carl to become the compassionate teacher he was. He would never embarrass a student, be-littlle a student, or accuse anyone unfairly. And Carl swore to himself that he would never use sarcasm or innuendoes that would hurt. He knew what it felt like to be hurt by a teacher, by a friend, by a father.

Carl picked up the gun again.

CHAPTER 4

"Well," Ms. Glenstone began as she lovingly glanced around her classroom of young ninth graders, "So, my lovelies, we are coming to an end to our family unit and it's time for all of you to choose your project. I have a list up here on the board and you can see all of the choices that are available, so you will need to sign up by yourself or with no more than four in a group.

"Any questions?" Suddenly half a dozen hands went up. Raizel Glenstone smiled. She loved it when her class had questions because that meant they were completely engaged.

"Okay, let's start with Jáquan."

Jáquan smiled, his light green eyes twinkling mischievously. "Ahh, Ms. G., can I sign up with someone from another class? You know I got a girlfriend in period 1 and she says that she can…"

"No, Jáquan, let me interrupt you right there. I cannot

allow you to work with someone from another class because you need to present your project together. Nice try though, Romeo." Raizel smiled. She knew that the old trick of letting kids work from different periods meant she lost total control of who was actually doing the work.

Piper shook her head from side to side, her long brown hair dancing on her back as though it had a life of its own. Her fingers were air-playing notes on her piano while she waited impatiently for Ms. Glenstone to call on her. She closed her large copper eyes praying silently to be called upon next.

Raizel sighed. The room was stifling warm with so many bodies fidgeting in their chairs while fumbling secretly with their cell phones on their laps pretending they were paying attention.

Raizel stared at Piper. She was such a drama queen, thought Raizel. "Okay, Piper. What's your question?"

Piper sat up abruptly, and opened her eyes as her raised hand slapped the desk hard in response to having to wait so long.

"Well, Ms. Glenstone, thank you for calling on me. I didn't have to wait very long this time around. Anyways, my question for you is, well, I don't want to sound too trendy, but we have not really, as far as I can tell…"

"Hmmmm, Piper, please get to the question, dear."

Piper shook her head as if she had just been slapped.

"Puleeeze, Ms. Glenstone, if you insist. I just felt it necessary to sorta tell you a bit more about my thought process before I go ahead and blurt out my question, but obviously, you are in a hurry today. I want to know why you do not have anything about transgenders or the other *bi* word on your fabulous list. I mean after all, it's all the news especially in *People* and on my Facebook page and of course Instagram, and if you must know I have observed quite a bit of this topic on my TikTok page, too!"

Raizel's shoulders sagged a bit. She looked around the room at all her little darlings anxiously awaiting an answer to such a brand-new and obviously very trendy topic. The subject matter was so incredibly hot off the presses that she did not have anything in her curriculum guide to help her with this.

Raizel clasped her hands together, took a deep breath, and looked straight into Piper's wide-open and seemingly innocent eyes. "Yes, Piper," she exhaled, "of course you can do your project on transgender, but please understand that we have gone over and over the concept of real facts versus social media gossip. I expect you to use only those resources that are from a reliable source, and to that end, you will have to verify your sources with me prior to presenting. Do I make myself crystal clear on this?"

Piper shrugged. She whispered to herself, soft enough that only a few students around her could hear as she hissed, "Yeah, clear as mud!"

Before Raizel could take another breath, there were more hands in the air than at a basketball game.

"Okay, let's see, Tommy, what's your question? Short one, I hope?"

Tommy laughed, but Tommy laughed at everything at

first. His voice was becoming deeper since the beginning of the semester and Raizel smiled making sure that she was not going to embarrass him when his voice cracked occasionally.

"Ms. Glenstone, my favorite teacher of all time, can I work on crazy football players who lost their shi…., I mean lost their cool because of too many concussions?" Tommy's multi-colored braces created a tiny rainbow around his smile as the fluorescent lights in the ceiling reflected on his face.

"Hmmmmm. I really like that topic for you, Tommy. And if you get deep into your research, feel free to add other sports if that happens to show up. Okay?"

Tommy pounded his chest in triumph. "Oh, yeah! Oh, yeah. I'm da man!"

The class broke out laughing because Tommy was such a goofy guy, but he had such a large heart. His brown eyes had gold specks in them and they sparkled with delight under his thick eyebrows.

"Okay, who else?" Raizel looked around the room, landing for a moment on Shaynee. Shaynee looked up at Raizel and immediately shifted her eyes to the floor. Raizel took the tacit *'don't call on me, please'* and continued to look around the room.

Lucas suddenly raised his hand. Raizel almost missed him since Lucas had taken the liberty of always sitting in the back of the room with his head down during most of the class time.

Raizel took a slow deep breath and let it out, counting

silently to five before calling on Lucas. She was unsure of his emotional state most of the time and felt that Lucas was a quiet ticking bomb who could explode at any given trigger.

"Yes, Lucas? You have a question?"

Lucas stood up. He looked at the clock on the wall and knew the bell was about to ring, but he was going to speak.

"I want…I want…I want…." Lucas shifted his body from side to side, his brown curly hair swirling around his neck. Raizel made a mental note to herself that Lucas appeared to have given up getting his hair cut since, oh dear God, since when? She chastised herself silently for not remembering because Lucas was so in tune with his physical appearance and, yes, lately, he looked, well, almost slovenly.

"Yes, Lucas, go on," she urged him hurriedly before the bell would ring.

There were a few murmurs and soft comments that were indistinguishable as the students were trying to figure out what Lucas wanted to ask.

"I want to find out…., well, I want to find out the truth as to how come Mr. DeWitt is not in our school anymore. I want to know what he did wrong and if there is a topic on that list of yours that fits him, I want to present the facts 'cause I think someone is lying their ass off. Uhhhh, sorry, Ms. Glenstone.

"You got a lot of topics, Ms. Glenstone, and I think I know which one I could use to find out the truth. That is if you'll let me."

And just like that, the bell rang, and everyone scampered to grab their book bags and whoosh, they were out the door.

Raizel fell into her chair, slumped more like it, and rested her forehead on her hands, her frizzy hair falling loosely around her ears as though she had just been in a fight over a hair do. *Where* **was** *Carl DeWitt? Somebody knows something but it's not me. Rumors from him dying from cancer to moving to Alaska to him marrying a student from another school.* Raizel shook her head, releasing more frizzy wisps of hair. She was frustrated and needed to talk to someone.

CHAPTER 5

Neva slowly closed the door to her classroom and turned around to see her after-school students staring up at her, questioning, concerned, curious. She looked at each one slowly as she was mentally taking roll and assessing their emotional state of being: Jilly, Cindy, Shaynee, Piper, Lucas (OMG he showed up today!), Linette, Jáquan, Whitney, Max, Tommy, Sofia, and Mateo. All twelve present and accounted for.

Now what do I do? I know the curriculum that Carl and I created; I know what has to be taught. What I don't know is how to tell them I don't know when Carl will be coming back or worse if he will come back. I'm tired of not knowing what's going on. And I know these kids want the truth; they don't want some lame excuse or explanation of what is going on.

"Good afternoon, my wonderful and fabulously delightful dozen. This is our last meeting till after break, so I want to go over some important scenarios with you."

Max raised his hand. The letter M was skillfully carved into the side of his scalp with his new haircut and his Afro was newly shaped. Max rarely drew attention to himself, but recently he had found some new confidence, hence the new 'do' and his increased levels of engagement in the program.

"Yes, Max. What's your question so early in today's session?"

"Well, you see Mrs. Waverly," Max was about to continue, but he hesitated as he looked at Lucas as though he were asking for permission to go on, "I'm just been wondering where Mr. DeWitt is at? I mean, it's been some months now and nobody knows nothing."

Neva automatically corrected, "Anything."

"Yeah, anything…whatever. So, like, what's up with that? What's going on? Can you tell us?"

Max looked around to see the reactions from his peers. They were all nodding their heads vigorously up and down. Everyone that is, except Lucas who was glaring at Max. Everyone knew that Lucas had asked the same question in health class and now Max was asking. Lucas's eyes seemed to be spitting nails at Max for taking away his concern as his own. Besides, everyone knew Lucas did not want to be in the group, and he only came now and then and even when he was here, he wasn't really here. Lucas was, well, Lucas, and everyone accepted him for who he was – that is whatever he was.

Max ignored the threatening glares from Lucas. If Lucas was not going to engage this afternoon, well, Max thought it was his turn to play the hero checking on their missing teacher.

Neva took a deep breath. She knew this was coming. She just did not know how to respond no matter how many times she replayed this exact question in her head. Her sea-green eyes suddenly filled with tears, and she bent her head down and stared at her hands, examining her cracked knuckles as if seeing them for the very first time. Her silver-streaked hair, normally pulled back in a bun, seemed to magically defy the navy blue ribbon it was wrapped around, and spilled over her shoulders.

Neva looked at her charges. "Max. And really to every one of you in here today, you have been so incredibly awesome, so understanding, so, well… enough of my accolades. You want answers. Well, guess what?" Neva suddenly raised her voice and in so doing shocked her students who never heard Neva act out in anger as she cried out, "So do I!"

Suddenly, there was a collective 'whoa' from the entire group as they were completely stunned to hear their teacher lose her temper.

"And so," Neva continued in a passionate tone, "here is my answer and it's the whole truth. I don't know! I don't God Damn know why Mr. DeWitt is not here, and I'll be damned if I am going to give you some fairy tale explanation to satisfy the administration and make you happy. But I'll tell you this, my darlings, we go on break in a couple of days, and I will make it my sworn duty to find out where Mr. DeWitt is and when he is coming back here. And that will be my gift to you!

"Okay? Max, and everyone else, and that includes Lucas,

who might not be looking at me, but I know he hears me, and all will be right with the world, I hope, and I promise you! And now let's get on with our business of the day."

Whitney stood up and yelled, "You go, Mrs. Waverly. You are the woman! I can rest easy now. Okay…okay… okay." And Whitney, flushed with excitement at her outburst, sat down as quickly as she had jumped up.

Neva smiled. She loved this part of her job. These were the moments that made all her hard work worthwhile because this was what she was destined to do in her life. She never found the time to meet that someone special, well she had but she pushed that memory back quickly. She never had the opportunity to have her own children, and again, a small nugget of a blurred memory slipped out into her consciousness, but she shoved it back. In the end, she felt that each year she had given birth, and it was her job to guide "her babies" to their highest potential. And although there were times when she felt she should have made that special partner work out, and could have become an official mother, well, sometimes things were not always in the cards. So, she was content to vicariously raise these children, one class period at a time for as long as she could be with them over the course of their four short high school years.

"Okay, one and all, let's move our desks into our special circle and get cracking on today's activity. Before we begin, however, I want to read you something very special to me. It is titled *Please Hear What I'm Not Saying* by Charles Finn. There is a copy of what I am going to read to you underneath your desk should you want to read along. Your choice, of course."

Neva read out loud to the group:

Don't be fooled by me.
Don't be fooled by the face I wear
for I wear a mask, a thousand masks,
masks that I'm afraid to take off,
and none of them is me.

Pretending is an art that's second nature with me,
but don't be fooled,
for God's sake don't be fooled.
I give you the impression that I'm secure,
that all is sunny and unruffled with me, within as well as without,
that confidence is my name and coolness my game,
that the water's calm and I'm in command
and that I need no one,
but don't believe me.
My surface may seem smooth but my surface is my mask,
ever-varying and ever-concealing.
Beneath lies no complacence.
Beneath lies confusion, and fear, and aloneness.
But I hide this. I don't want anybody to know it.
I panic at the thought of my weakness exposed.
That's why I frantically create a mask to hide behind,
a nonchalant sophisticated facade,
to help me pretend,
to shield me from the glance that knows.

But such a glance is precisely my salvation, my only hope,
and I know it.
That is, if it's followed by acceptance,
if it's followed by love.
It's the only thing that can liberate me from myself,
from my own self-built prison walls,
from the barriers I so painstakingly erect.
It's the only thing that will assure me
of what I can't assure myself,
that I'm really worth something.
But I don't tell you this. I don't dare to, I'm afraid to.
I'm afraid your glance will not be followed by acceptance,
will not be followed by love.
I'm afraid you'll think less of me,
that you'll laugh, and your laugh would kill me.
I'm afraid that deep-down I'm nothing
and that you will see this and reject me.

So I play my game, my desperate pretending game,
with a facade of assurance without
and a trembling child within.
So begins the glittering but empty parade of masks,
and my life becomes a front.
I idly chatter to you in the suave tones of surface talk.
I tell you everything that's really nothing
and nothing of what's everything,
of what's crying within me.
So when I'm going through my routine
do not be fooled by what I'm saying.

Please listen carefully and try to hear what I'm not saying,
what I'd like to be able to say,
what for survival I need to say,
but what I can't say.

I don't like hiding.
I don't like playing superficial phony games.
I want to stop playing them.
I want to be genuine and spontaneous and me
but you've got to help me.
You've got to hold out your hand
even when that's the last thing I seem to want.
Only you can wipe away from my eyes
the blank stare of the breathing dead.
Only you can call me into aliveness.
Each time you're kind, and gentle, and encouraging,
each time you try to understand because you really care,
my heart begins to grow wings –
very small wings,
very feeble wings,
but wings!

With your power to touch me into feeling
you can breathe life into me.
I want you to know that.
I want you to know how important you are to me,
how you can be a creator – an honest-to-God creator –
of the person that is me
if you choose to.

You alone can break down the wall behind which I tremble,
you alone can remove my mask,
you alone can release me from my shadow-world of panic,
from my lonely prison,
if you choose to.
Please choose to.

Do not pass me by.
It will not be easy for you.
A long conviction of worthlessness builds strong walls.
The nearer you approach to me the blinder I may strike back.
It's irrational, but despite what the books say about man
often I am irrational.
I fight against the very thing I cry out for.
But I am told that love is stronger than strong walls
and in this lies my hope.
Please try to beat down those walls
with firm hands but with gentle hands
for a child is very sensitive.

Who am I, you may wonder?
I am someone you know very well.
For I am every man you meet
and I am every woman you meet.

Neva put the paper down and closed her eyes. She wanted to give the group a few moments of silence to process what she had just read. She heard a few sniffles, and with her eyes still closed reached behind her to her desk, grabbed the box of Kleenex, and handed it to Linette who was sitting next to her.

Neva waited a few more moments till the Kleenex box worked its way back to her. She opened her eyes.

"I want to talk about this, but not yet. I want it to settle into you, marinate for a while and we'll get back to it. For right now, I want to transition to the main activity."

Neva passed around white cardstock papers and several plastic bins filled with markers, crayons, and colored pencils.

"Take one sheet of the cardstock. Yes, you will notice that the papers are not whole; they look cut out, and that's on purpose. So just select one and then grab whatever marking utensil you choose as you pass the bins of writing tools. You can grab a variety of different ones. Just because you take a blue crayon doesn't mean you cannot take a pencil and a marker. Be bold. Be creative. Be adventurous. Because one thing we do not do in this room is judge. Have fun with your choices. That's what this is all about. And ultimately, my loveys, that is what your life will be about – the choices that you make."

The plastic bins were passed around and each student chose their tools, taking time to look at their selections, tossing back some, repicking, and rethinking. This was serious business for them, and they did not take this task lightly.

Neva raised an eyebrow as she watched with silent joy when Lucas grabbed a handful of crayons and markers and a few colored pencils and studied each one as though his life depended upon his array of various writing tools.

Once everyone had their paper and their drawing utensils in front of them, Neva gave her directions.

"Here we go. In front of you is a blank piece of cardstock. It's strong even though it's only paper. It's empty right now because you will be filling it. Feel free to use any and all of the crayons, markers, and colored pencils wherever you choose to on this paper. And now for the directions, and please, no whining that you cannot draw, cannot color, or cannot create. No judgy, no criticisms, and surely no laughter because we all know how we've been hurt before.

"Okay? First step is to find a little tiny pencil mark of the letter *t*. I have already placed that mark on your paper. That is where the top of your paper needs to be. Turn your paper till that little *t* is near the top of your desk. There are going to be five portions of your paper. And the first one needs to go in the middle. That is, wherever the middle of your paper is. Ready? Here we go now."

Neva stopped. She looked around making sure all twelve students were with her. They were looking at her, questioning their next steps. That was a good thing, thought Neva. Always question. Do not take life for granted she begged silently, knowingly.

Twelve students in a circle. Each with their own baggage. Each with their own drama, insecurities, and dreams. And Neva wanted to make sure she was building their confidence all the while encouraging those dreams to continue growing and hopefully becoming a reality.

Neva continued, "Now, let's begin by drawing a picture of you in the middle. The picture of you can be a stick figure if you are so inclined, a cartoon image of yourself, or as close to a real image as you possibly can draw. Again, use any of the tools you picked out of the bin. Feel free to come grab more drawing implements or switch out what you currently have if you feel the need.

"After you draw yourself, I want you to write underneath your picture the weather forecast that describes your personality. Yes, think about how the weatherman describes a typical day, a day that in essence describes you to a tee! From hurricanes to sleet to sunny or windy or any combination you can think of that shouts 'this is me' warts and all!"

There was some giggling and a few "oh nos" along with some big smiles to go along with their thought patterns. Neva knew their brains were on full speed ahead modality and she could see their eyes twinkling as their heads were filling up with all kinds of thoughts and expressions.

"Next, and now you can use any part of the paper for the next few parts. Please draw for me your hobby or hobbies or your sport or your sports that you love. Feel free to draw one or more of these if you wish."

Neva waited for a few minutes as her students were so engaged, they barely looked up when she began directing again.

"And I know you are busy working, creating, thinking, but I have a few more directions for you," Neva interrupted her group. "I want you to draw something that represents your family life, how you see it, how you feel it, what it looks like, or even what you hope it looks like."

Neva looked around the room carefully making sure she had not touched too sensitive a chord. She recognized that she was always on the edge of pushing one of the students too far, creating a sudden meltdown, or causing a brief acting out that could get ugly. She looked for body cues, facial expressions, or sudden grunts or sniffles.

She felt confident moving on as she stated, "And then, lastly, create in a drawing or words or a song or a poem how you visualize your dreams and your goals for your future. I'm going to leave you to this on your own, but I will walk around so I can answer any of your questions one-on-one. Alright, my little afternoon munchkins, go to it!"

CHAPTER 6

Beverly packed up her school bag and surveyed her classroom. All the labs were straightened and cleaned. The glass vials sparkled, and the numerous metal containers reflected shiny crystals from the overhead lighting. All was right with her world as she inspected her room. This was her control center. She was in charge, and no one was there to slap her around or make her feel inferior. She sat down in her chair and sighed. There were so many rumors floating around the building, and she did not want to be a part of the drama. She had enough of her own drama these past few months.

Beverly took out her cell phone and texted Alisa, her only friend in the entire building. For some reason, Beverly sensed that the other staff members distanced themselves from her. She wasn't sure exactly, but there was a tension that was so thick you could cut it with a butter knife. And no matter how many times she asked Alisa to confide in her, Alisa was silent.

One morning as Beverly strolled into the teacher's lounge, Sam Tannereck and Raizel Glenstone got up from the sofa, gathered their belongings, and walked out. Beverly was about to say hello and what's new, guys, but the two of them kept their heads together whispering as they left. Beverly grunted as they passed her, but they completely ignored her.

"It's your loss," Beverly said to no one since the lounge was now empty of any staff members. "I'm going to just enjoy some peace and quiet without having to listen to any of you whine about your students."

Beverly had been staying at Alisa's home for the last few months and even though the two of them had long talks about nothing significant, the subject of Carl never came up. Alisa refused to discuss the situation and Beverly did not want to destroy their friendship which had become as fragile as a swatch of gossamer fabric. Alisa would make dinner; they would eat in silence or sometimes discuss the weather or some sales for the upcoming Christmas season. But once dinner was completed and the kitchen cleaned, Alisa would say she had work to do in her office, and that was the last Beverly would see her for the evening.

After school that day, Beverly was still obsessing over Sam and Raizel walking out of the lounge. She knew she needed to let it go, but for some reason she was still bothered by it.

Alone in her classroom, Beverly thought so much about her current situation between the cold distance she felt with Alisa, to the way the staff was treating her. She reached a point where she was clenching her fists and banging them on the desk without her realizing it. She was filled with anger, but she wasn't sure where to lay the blame.

Beverly stood up, pushing her chair so hard it flipped over on the floor, and lay there, the wheels on the legs spinning almost as fast as her thoughts.

"I hate everyone. I hate that jerk Carl because he has caused everyone here to hate me; I hate everyone on my team; I hate Alisa and I hate Ted. Today is it. I'm done with all of this. I need to go back home and deal with Ted and finalize my life and move on. I can't be a charity case with Alisa anymore. And Ted is going to see a Beverly he has never seen before. Not even my father would recognize me."

Beverly choked back a sob when she thought of her father. Now why did I even think of him, she thought to herself. The last time I visited his grave I spit on it and I will gladly do it again.

Beverly, walking around her room as a Queen would stroll through her private sanctuary, pulled out her cell phone from her pocket. She scrolled down through her text messages and found the latest thread she had written to Alisa. Alisa had never even responded which fueled Beverly's anger to another level. Beverly gritted her teeth, squinted her eyes, and typed out her message slowly. She did not want any auto-type to create a flowery message. She was too angry to be nice anymore. She read her message to herself to be sure.

Hey, girl…I won't be coming by today after school. There are some things I need to set straight at home with Ted. Uhhh, I'll come by sometime this week to pick up my clothes and stuff. Thanks for everything, Alisa. You were truly my BFF. Don't call me. Later, B

Beverly hesitated over her choice of words. Are you still my BFF she thought or is that now in the past? I'm thinking it's in the past and that's how I'm going to leave you and our friendship.

Satisfied, Beverly stopped stomping around the room, took off her lab coat, and hung it up on the back of her door. She slipped her phone into her pants pocket, scooped up her bag, grabbed her winter coat, and walked out of her classroom. She turned left, heading in the wrong direction from the parking lot, but she wanted to accidentally, more like surreptitiously, stroll by Neva's classroom.

"I know I'm just punishing myself for doing this," Beverly whispered to herself. "Be brave, be fearless, and add in some courage also," she chuckled out loud, but as she did, she turned her head in all directions to ensure no one witnessed her actions.

But her evil laughter was swallowed as Beverly approached Neva's classroom. She heard the students talking and giggling and the movement of chairs and desks. Suddenly, Beverly could not control herself any longer. She stood outside the classroom door, hesitated for just a split second, and then flung the door open.

There was immediate silence. The students froze in mid speak and stared at her.

Neva looked up from her desk, looked over at the students, and said as convincingly as she could muster, "It's all right, group. Continue with your project and I will see what Mrs. Winewrought wants this afternoon."

Neva got up slowly and deliberately and marched assertively to the door, stopping only inches away from Beverly's face. Neva would not be intimated by this woman, and she was tired of Beverly's stares and tacit accusations of Neva and Carl running the program. Neva had overheard from a few teachers who were receiving long accusatory texts from Beverly blaming Neva and Carl for stealing what was rightfully Beverly's ideas. It was a false narrative, and everyone knew it but Beverly.

"Beverly, Mrs. Winewrought," said Neva in a sweet but firm tone not backing away from Beverly. "What can I do for you? Please, let's step outside my door, as my students are very engaged at the moment in a project." And with that, Neva placed her hand on Beverly's shoulder and gently guided her outside her classroom.

Beverly stiffened her shoulders and shrugged them in an attempt to shake off Neva's firm grip. "I want to see what you are doing in there, Neva. I have a right to see what I was denied," spat Beverly, her tone dripping in venom. "I demand that you allow me in there. I was supposed to be in charge of this program, and you stole it from me! You cheated me out of something I deserved. Something I worked so hard to get and it's not fair! It's just not fair. Now you let me in there and I mean right now!"

Beverly's voice got louder and higher pitched and she was losing her breath from being overly excited. She shoved Neva aside and thrust herself upon the closed door reaching for the doorknob and jerking it from side to side to yank it open when suddenly a male voice bellowed from down the hall.

"Hey, excuse me! I said, HEY!" Scott Sheldrake's strong deep baritone shouts reverberated in outrage, and it shook Beverly's focus. She let go of the door handle and slowly, carefully turned towards Scott.

Scott had raced down the hallway and was now standing face to face with Beverly putting himself in the middle and blocking Neva for safety's sake.

Scott needed to assess the situation immediately. He was the lead security guard for Wells, a retired policeman and he had a sixth sense for recognizing that this was not a friendly conversation occurring in the hallway. He had known Neva for many years and never once had she had an issue with any student or staff member. Scott stood staring at Beverly, his feet in a wide stance and his hands held out ready to grab Beverly if necessary. In a demanding strong voice, he asked Neva, "Mrs. Waverly, what's going on here?"

Neva looked at Scott with pleading eyes as though she could communicate with him via telepathy. "Oh, Mr.

Sheldrake, Mrs. Winewrought just came by to say hello and when she realized she had interrupted something very important happening in my classroom, I escorted her into the hallway so we could talk privately. I appreciate you being right here at this time and perhaps you could make sure Mrs. Winewrought can get to her car safely. She seems to be a bit distraught, and I am not sure why."

Beverly's head snapped up her lips curled up like a snake ready to strike. "I am not fucking distraught, you old hag! I am downright goddamned angry and pissed off at you and this whole frigging school!

"And no, Mr. Sheldrake, you do NOT need to escort me to my car. I can find my own God damn car by myself, thank you not at all! If I need a rent-a-cop I'll be sure to call on you!" Beverly wrenched her body around so that Scott was no longer within arm's length of her.

Beverly sneered at Neva, leaned over, spit at her feet, turned around, and marched triumphantly down the hall.

Neva gasped and looked at Scott. Scott immediately flew into the former police-in-pursuit mode, whipped out his walkie, and raced after Beverly but purposely kept a very close distance behind her. Beverly reached the exits, turned around, and snapped at Scott, "What? Are you going to arrest me for leaving the building? C'mon, Scott, you're better than this. Leave me the fuck alone. I didn't do anything to Nothing Neva."

Scott, sucking in air, bent over with his hands on his knees and his head tilted up looking at Beverly. He was staring at her as if seeing this woman for the very first time.

"What's going on, Beverly? Neva didn't do anything to you. Now, c'mon. You *spit* at her? Really? You spit at another adult like a spoiled brat."

Beverly held the door open ready to dash out should Scott approach her. He was keeping his distance, but she did not want to take any chances.

"Oh, like you know so much, Scott. You know everything that's going on in this building. You and PC think you have the corner on all the goings on around here. Well, take it from me, bub, you don't know Jack! Wait! Let me rephrase that for ya. You don't know Carl! And that's a fact."

Scott felt as though Beverly's vindictive words had sliced him right through the gut. Why was she bringing in his partner, Pauline Clifton? PC, as everyone called her, did know the pulse of the school and he was certainly going to talk to her tomorrow about this. PC knew every student and their issues for the most part, and she knew most of the teachers as well. Everyone confided in PC, but it seems, everyone but Beverly.

But, Carl? What did she know about Carl and his situation? Scott, acting somewhat detached and nonchalant, using his best sympathetic tone uttered, his brown eyes softened as she said gently, "Beverly, what about Carl? Am I missing something here? Do you want to talk about it? Did Carl do something to you that I don't know about? Did he hurt you? Did he say anything to you?" Scott had worked in the sex criminal division for many years and while his radar was being tugged at here, it wasn't raising any real flags. Not with Carl, anyway.

But Beverly refused to take the bait. She laughed, a low, flat sound emanating from deep within her, "Like I said, Scott, you think you know everything, but baby, this one is out of your league." And with that, she let go of the door and strutted jubilantly towards her car cackling loudly to herself.

Scott followed her with his eyes but did not pursue her. He shook his head from side to side in confusion and turned around and went back to check on Mrs. Waverly.

CHAPTER 7

Carl said goodbye to Lemont Jacobs and laid his cell phone gently down on the desk. Lemont had been representing him since the beginning of his worst nightmare and the two of them had become friends. Well, thought Carl, as good a friend as one can have when it was forged through a lie that he has had to prove otherwise.

The Glock was still in Carl's lap. He was not going to use it. He thought about it. Thought long and hard. *What kind of person would others think of me if I were to use this Glock and end my life? I would forever be labeled as guilty. And I am not! I am not guilty of any wrongdoing, and I'll be damned if I give in to the lies and the fabrications. Lemont believes me. And he believes in me and together we will fight the ugly accusations – whatever they are and whomever spread them!*

Carl reached over and picked over his dad's collection of pens and pencils. They were neatly arranged on the desk next to a pile of empty pads of papers from various organizations. Some of the pads had his dad's name and address on them, but mostly they were freebies from donations to every organization who reached out to his father. His father, for all his faults, was magnanimous; he gave to every charity no matter how small. It was his way of proving to himself perhaps that he was a decent human being. *Too bad he wasn't that decent to me*, thought Carl.

Carl picked up a new pen and ripped off one of the sheets from a pretty blue pad of paper. Carl jotted down the name and number of his next interview that Lemont had shared with him. He did not recognize the name of the person he was going to speak to regarding the false allegations, but he knew this individual was somebody high up in the echelon of the county. Lemont would meet Carl at the designated office next week and there Carl would have one more opportunity to tell his side of the story. This interview would be his last. Carl prayed that this individual would see Carl for who he was and what he stood for and that he was innocent, completely innocent of any wrongdoing. Carl knew that this was his last chance because this person would be the very last person who would hear him. And then that was it. A decision would be made and then Carl would be able to take the next step in his life. Whatever that step would be.

But before next week, Carl had some things he had to do, some things he needed to sort out, and honestly, he was ready. He picked up the Glock and fondled it in his hands. *It's so heavy in its evilness. Yes, I understand if you are hunting or defending your life, but by itself, I see the harm it can do; the sadness it can cause; the hurt that will last long past the life of the cold black steel instrument.*

Suddenly, the front door burst open. Carl almost dropped the gun on the floor.

"What the fu…?" said Carl out loud.

"Carl?! Carl! Where are you?"

Carl stood up, the revolver still grasped in his hand, and shouted, "Hey, who? And there in front of him stood Chip, his brother. Chip had the same deep brown hair as Carl, but with peacock blue eyes that always seemed to twinkle.

Chip's eyes immediately flew to the gun that was dangling on Carl's side. His eyes darkened and his mouth opened wide with shock, and he held his arms up over his head.

Chip pleaded softly, "Carl… dude… brother… c'mon, man, lay that weapon down. I'm not going to hurt you and I sure as hell don't want you to hurt yourself. Or me. You're not going to hurt yourself, are you? Carl, please, put that down, man."

Carl stared at Chip. He had not heard from his brother in months. They had not spoken a single word or texted with one another. They were no longer close ever since Emma, well, ever since Emma died. The two of them never talked about the incident. Never talked about their parents Harry and Leila or anything important. According to Carl, Chip was the hero of the family, and heroes did not need to explain their actions nor were they capable of hearing others because everyone else was just weak by comparison.

Chip walked slowly towards Carl and Carl, as if in a

dream, seemed to move in slow motion. And then something inside him clicked. He looked down at his arm like it belonged to another human being. He took a deep breath and carefully, methodically, and deliberately placed the Glock on the desk. He looked up at Chip.

"Hey, Chip."

"Man! That's all you got to say to me? Where the hell have you been? I've been trying to reach you for damn, I don't know how long. I left messages on your cell phone. I even dropped by your school to see if I could find you there and they…they…some lady in the office…shit, Carl, why didn't you tell me you've been suspended from your job? What the hell has been going on with you?"

"What do you want me to say to you, Chip? That your brother is an utter failure…again. I can't even stay in a job I love without screwing that up, too. Look, man, you may be my brother, but hell, you have never been there for me. So why now? Why are you suddenly running into Mom and Dad's house looking for me like you are even interested in my well-being?"

Chip stared at Carl as if seeing him for the first time. Chip noticed that Carl had not shaved in, well, it looked like weeks. And his eyes, they used to shine like chestnuts on fire and now they were dull and washed out. His clothes were hanging off his brother like a mismatched mannequin. Carl had lost weight and Chip, even though he hadn't seen his brother in, hell, it had to have been since a year ago Christmas, he looked like a raggedy Andy thrown in a corner unloved.

"It's mom, Carl. She's in the hospital. She had a heart attack. At least that's what the doctors said. She's resting comfortably, but she's been asking for you. Constantly. Not me, Carl. You. Only you. Dad is not doing well, either, but you know him. He's either drunk or yelling at the world. He's no use to mom right now.

"I've been trying to get in touch with you so we could both go to the hospital. You and me. It's gonna be a long drive since Mom and Dad like their condo so far in the south. Can you come with me?"

Carl looked at his phone. He needed to let Lemont know he would be out of town for a while. But, damn, he had his interview coming up soon. It didn't matter. Not much in his life mattered right now. But his mom was his priority right now. Carl stood up, scooped up the Glock gently into his hand, walked over to the safe and placed it gingerly inside, closed the door with a soft thud, turned the combination lock several times, and turned to his brother who was watching Carl as though he were a stranger.

"Let's go, Chip. I just need to lock up the house and we're outta here."

CHAPTER 8

Neva was beaming with pride. Her group had just presented their pictures of who they were and their hobbies and their ambitions and she could not have been happier. She just sat there and stared at them, her heart bursting with love for their honesty and their hopes for a future filled with wonder and joy.

"Wow! I am so thrilled with your artwork! And, Max! Who knew you were such an artist! And Jáquan, I love the picture of you and your brothers – so awesome! Linette, yikes, I cannot wait to try some of your special recipes that were handed down to you from your family.

"Mateo, I am in love with your dog. You will have to bring him here one day so I can bring my Atticus along and they can have a play date! Deal? Hah hah!"

The students were laughing and nudging one another as they enjoyed sharing their stories.

"But you didn't think this was the end of this project, did you?" questioned Neva. "Oh, no my little caterpillars longing to transform. We still have one more piece of this. Are you ready?"

Neva looked around the room reading their faces. They were tired. It was way past the end of the school day, and they had given Neva everything they had. They shrugged in unison; they did not want to disappoint.

"Oh, my, oh, my, how quickly we are losing that surge of energy you all bounced in here with. Okay, last thing of the day. I want you to take your lovely, and I do mean lovely, creations of who you are and, did you happen to notice that all of your papers have funny little cuts and bends on them?"

"Oh, yeah, I did," called out Mateo. "I thought maybe you ran outta paper and these were the only scraps you had left for us to use."

"No she didn't," chimed Whitney, her strawberry blonde hair unraveling from its early morning braid, "Of course Mrs. Waverly had a plan. You did have a plan, didn't you, Mrs. Waverly?

Neva laughed. Leave it to Whitney to feel like she knew the answer but needed validation to be absolutely sure.

Jilly spoke up. "Uhhh, guys, did you think for a second that maybe, just maybe these pieces all kinda fit together like some puzzle?" Jilly was one of the smartest in their small group. She rarely spoke of her family, being the youngest of five with her twin brothers over ten years older than she was. It embarrassed her and caused her to keep those feelings close to the vest.

There were murmurings and some 'duhs' spoken outloud.

"Yes, Jilly. You hit the nail right on the proverbial head. If you would look at your, yes, your piece of the puzzle and head over to the back wall which you will see, is completely empty right now. I want you to figure out how to put all of your pieces together so that the puzzle will magically come together to form a beautiful picture.

"Now, go on, get up and let's see how you can problem solve this one."

Neva waited. She wanted to see who would take charge. Who would ask for tape? Who would organize the group? Who would just hand over their paper to someone else and go sit down and isolate? Who would assist? Who would criticize? So many questions with so many answers that would truly define these kids.

Neva sat back and watched and studied. Shaynee handed her paper to Jilly and went back to her seat. Neva thought about Shaynee's drawings. She drew a beautiful picture of her mother, but her father's face was turned away as though she did not want to fill in the features. But why?

And, of course, Whitney and Tommy took charge. No surprise there. Sofia rummaged in the materials boxes for tape and Lucas busied himself with cutting off pieces of the tape. Piper was excited to point and direct where she thought the pieces needed to go and Jáquan loved pounding the taped pieces to the wall. Linette quietly assisted and Max was busy whispering something to Cindy who kept nodding her head up and down in agreement. Mateo was gathering all the various crayons and markers and colored pencils and organizing them in their special plastic bins for Neva.

Neva sighed. All was right with the world. These kids were going to be just fine. She smiled and sat back and watched the magic unfold.

• • •

Beverly pressed down hard on her accelerator. She was sick and tired of not being believed. She had planted the seed that Carl DeWitt was a horrible, inappropriate teacher who crossed the line with students and even though he had been sent packing, the school's collective mindset seemed to be in his court.

This wasn't the first time Beverly had sowed evil seeds. She wasn't quite sure why she did it the very first time. Wow, she started reminiscing. I think it was in high school. Yes, she was sure of it. She did not like her English teacher, what was his name? Oh, yeah, Mr. O'Sullivan. He was young, and handsome and he liked boys. She was sure of it because he would never call on the girls in her class. And she was used to being a shining star in her classes and this time it wasn't happening. So she thought she would just start a little rumor. Nothing big, nothing too serious, but a rumor nonetheless. And it stuck.

When she met with her counselor to go over her schedule for the following semester, she slipped that she refused to have Mr. O'Sullivan as her teacher because, well, you know, she said, he always has boys in his room during lunch and oh, yes, she recalled to her counselor, he also happened to have them in his car after school. She knew that for a fact. Well, it was a fact in her imagination at any rate.

Beverly knew the counselor would pass that on to administration and sure enough, Mr. O'Sullivan was suddenly replaced with a long-term old female substitute who always called on Beverly for the answers. Years later she had heard from some old classmates that Mr. O'Sullivan had quit teaching and moved to the West Coast.

From that point on in Beverly's life, whenever she felt threatened or disliked someone, she managed to embellish and fabricate a scenario that always ended with Beverly smiling. She promised herself that living with a father who was mean and abusive only taught her how to plan her revenge on every male she despised.

"Sure," she said to herself in the car as her mind returned her to the parking lot at Wells, "Sure, be on Team Carl. Let's see where that loser takes you in the end."

Beverly was so filled with hatred and jealousy that it drove her to her next move. She had texted Alisa that she would not be coming back to partake in Alisa's hospitality, generous though it was. Beverly knew she could not be Alisa's roommate forever. She had a house. She had a husband and she needed to deal with Ted. In a heartless conversation with Ted, she finally told him that he was an inadequate spouse and she wanted to end their marriage.

Beverly threatened to file charges of physical and emotional abuse against Ted and expose him for what he truly was – incompetent and insignificant to her, but Beverly knew she would never go that far. She did not have the courage to do that. It was easier to destroy a colleague, someone who she would never see again, but in a rare touch of regret and guilt, she accepted that there were times when she pushed Ted too far. In a sudden change of heart, Beverly thought that perhaps they could still find a way to stay together. After all, she thought, we had talked about starting a family and maybe this would be the best way for us to have a fresh start, a new beginning.

Beverly drove faster, ignoring the fact that she was driving a good 20 miles over the speed limit. Suddenly, a white light flashed twice in Beverly's rearview mirror. "Shit! I completely forgot about that speed camera! Damn it! If I wasn't already so pissed at everyone today, this just rocked me beyond all caring!"

Slowing the car to the correct speed limit, Beverly inhaled and exhaled with several slow breaths. She needed to be completely calm when she entered her house. She knew that if Ted was there, and she came on too strong right away, a fight would materialize like a sudden thunderstorm. Beverly needed to be focused and ready for anything from a meltdown to an explosion. She had to be sharp and not just outraged because that would only squash her true intentions.

Beverly turned the corner to her street. She reduced her

speed to a crawl as she suddenly noticed an unfamiliar car in her driveway.

"Who could that be? Maybe it's a loaner. Ted had been wanting to get some work done on the car so that could be the mysterious car. Maybe." But cold chills climbed up her neck and she absently grabbed the back of her head as though there was something tangible there, something she could squeeze the life out of and move on.

Beverly realized she was talking out loud again and pressed her lips tightly together until they felt numb. People will think I'm losing it if they see me shouting wildly in my car. Or then again, they are probably thinking I'm talking on my cell phone.

Beverly decided to park her car on the street. She shut off the engine, took a deep breath, and grabbed her school bag and the overnight bag that she had been keeping in the car. She always knew she wanted to come back home; she just wasn't sure when she would gather up the nerve to approach Ted. Would he be welcoming, or would he be resentful? Would he immediately instigate an argument, or would he embrace her in his arms and promise to love her forever?

Without looking back, Beverly clicked her remote to lock the car and plodded to the front door weighed down with her belongings along with a bit of self-doubt. This is silly, she thought. Why should I be so nervous about coming back? This is my house, too, after all. I belong here.

With more anger than confidence, Beverly snatched her

house key from her school bag and slid it smoothly into the lock. She turned the door handle, and instantly the aroma of something savory and delicious wafted into her nose and she smiled. Oh, my God, she thought ecstatically, Ted has finally learned how to cook. She smiled. This was not going to be a difficult homecoming she convinced herself, ignoring her earlier mixed feelings.

Beverly swung the door open all the way, and the sweet sounds of Alicia Keys playing on their Spotify lifted her spirits even higher. Ted had always complained about paying for music when he could get whatever music he wanted for free, but Beverly had insisted he sign with Spotify demanding that she wanted to be able to pick and choose her favorites especially when she and Ted disagreed on everything musical.

Beverly, having changed her attitude completely in those last few minutes, waltzed into her doorway feeling strong and hopeful and ready to proclaim her love for him and declare a strong apology for staying away so long, and praying he missed her as much as she missed him.

Beverly's shoes jammed into the flooring and she stopped suddenly. She heard the stranger's voice first. It sounded vaguely familiar, but Beverly couldn't quite place it. The voice was calling for Ted, but Beverly did not hear Ted's voice.

And then she heard him. "Hey, baby, I'm coming. Just wait a minute, honey." Was that Ted, her Ted? Was that his voice sounding so sickly sweet as though it was dripping with sugar? But who was he talking to?

Beverly dropped her satchel and her overnight bag on the floor with a loud thud and careened into the kitchen only to stop so abruptly she almost fell over.

"Who the fuck are you? And what are you doing in my kitchen?" Beverly spat accusatorily. Her words hissed angrily with venom as she queried this stranger.

The woman, tall, blonde with pouting lips that saw many a Botox session, smiled enabling her ultra-white teeth to sparkle in the kitchen light. "Why, hello. I'm Livvy. And you are?"

Beverly was nonplussed. "What do you mean who am I? I live here. Aren't you Ted's, what?"

And then it exploded on Beverly like someone had smacked her with a rock from a pea shooter. It was Ted's secretary. His secretary? Oh, no! Oh, shit! Oh, hell, no!

Like a deranged and wronged woman, Beverly said carefully, bitterly, and with controlled vindictiveness, "What are you doing here?"

Livvy smiled, her green eyes narrowing dangerously into slits. Her voice sounded like broken oyster shells crashing on a driveway as she responded cooly, "I believe that is going to be something Ted needs to share with you."

At that exact moment, Ted waltzed into the kitchen. The smile on his face dropped immediately. His head jerked from Livvy to Beverly and back to Livvy again. His mouth opened and instantly closed.

Ted took a few seconds to analyze his situation and slowly and deliberately said in a monotone, "Hello, Beverly. This is Livvy, Livvy Shields, my girlfriend.

CHAPTER 9

Shaynee sat in Raizel Glenstone's class. Yesterday in her special after-school group she had drawn a picture of herself, her family, her hobbies, and her personality described in weather-related terms. What had she said? A good chance of wicked tornadoes followed by freezing rain and possible rainbows. Is that who she was? All mixed up inside? Stormy? Frozen? Rainbows? Hahah. Where were the rainbows? She hadn't been able to find any in the last year and she wasn't getting any closer to finding them although as a dreamer she would keep trying.

Shaynee did not think of herself as beautiful. In her mind her long, thick deep mahogany curls were always in her way and her heart-shaped face with large milk-chocolate almond-shaped eyes only brought her to the realization that she did not look like anyone in her family. Not her mother, her father, or her identical twin brothers. At ten years old they had blond hair and hazel eyes like her mom and tall gangly legs like her dad. Shaynee's skin was not pale, but what did her mother say? That she was kissed by the sun before she was born so she had a glow that radiated. So where did Shaynee fit in with her family?

"Shaynee? Are you listening? Did you hear what I just said?" questioned Ms. Glenstone. She was very worried about Shaynee recently and even brought her up at her last team meeting. Unfortunately, Shaynee was not the sort of 'at risk' student who would cause most teachers to see a red flag flying. Shaynee was not a troublemaker; she earned great grades, and she was a teacher-pleaser. So why worry?

But Raizel had a special knack for seeing through kids to detect what lurked beneath the surface. She could sense when one of her students was hiding something, shoveling hurt deep down, fighting a hidden fear, or swallowing heavy, heart-pounding anxiety. Whether it was brought on by parents who were in the middle of their own crisis and not realizing the impact it was having on their children, or worse yet, whether it was from parents who were physically or emotionally abusing their children. Raizel's special sensitive barometer would convey all kinds of signals and she always listened to her gut.

And with Shaynee, it seemed to have developed only recently, but Raizel could tell. She could almost smell it when one of her students switched from everyday normal or goofy to suddenly quiet, withdrawn, distracted. Shaynee had become reclusive, a big flag in Raizel's mind. Secondly, and more importantly, Shaynee's grades had plummeted. Dropping a letter grade here or there was one thing but when you went from all A's sprinkled with an occasional B and then suddenly barely passing, then something really big was amiss.

Raizel was determined to find out what was going on with Shaynee especially since her team was not interested in pursuing this change in Shaynee. Raizel had just finished explaining who was going to present their projects when she noticed that Shaynee had spaced out. She was staring through the window and other than a few tree branches scattered with leftover snow that was still clinging to the hard wooden hands of the oaks, there was nothing of note outside. But Raizel could tell that Shaynee was not observing nature; she was deep in thought. So deep, she never heard Raizel calling on her.

The class period was ending, the students were packing up, grabbing their water bottles, and quickly checking their cell phones for any urgent news from their peers, but Shaynee was frozen in her chair.

The bell rang and Raizel said, "Goodbye, guys. Have a great day. Oh, Shaynee, could you please stay back a sec for me?"

Shaynee snapped her head up as if she were being smacked in the back of her neck. Her curls fell over her eyes and tears overflowed.

"I'm sorry, Ms. Glenstone," sobbed Shaynee spontaneously. "I don't know what's wrong with me today." Shaynee's shoulders slumped down and her head fell on her arms that were folded on the desk.

Raizel got up, pushed her chair aside, walked over to

Shaynee's desk, and sat down next to her. "It's okay, sweetheart. We all have days like these. But I'm here for you if you want to talk with me.

"Ummm, Shaynee, hon, by any chance do you think that completing your project for me has something to do with how you are feeling right now?"

Shaynee sniffed and wiped her nose with the back of her hand.

Raizel tried not to break into a smile. No matter how old these kids get, they never used a damn tissue she thought.

"I don't know, Ms. G, I uhh, I… can we kinda talk privately about this?"

Raizel looked around the room. It was empty. All the students had quickly dispersed leaving the two of them alone. "Sweetie, there's no one else in the room but you and me, right?"

Shaynee bobbed her head up and down. "Yeah, I know. But what I mean is, after I talk with you, can, uh, I don't know…do you need to tell anyone about this conversation is what I'm getting at?"

Raizel thought for a moment, her brain sifting through the file cabinets in her head looking for the rules. "Shaynee," Raizel said haltingly, "whatever we talk about right now, I need to know one really important thing. Are you in danger of hurting yourself – or anyone else?" Raizel knew she had to use her best discretion and was hoping that Shaynee was not in any physical danger.

Shaynee's wet eye spread wide open. "Oh, dear God, no, Ms. G., no way. I am not going to hurt myself or my mom or dad or the twins. No way would I… or could I? How could you ask me such a thing?"

"Well, Shaynee, if I thought in any way that you were going to hurt yourself, honey, then I am under legal obligation to report it. If your answer to me is no, then, please feel free to share with me what's going on. What's hurting you, baby? How can I help you?"

Shaynee took a deep breath that had her shoulders shuddering and her lips quivering. Raizel could see the thoughts shifting in Shaynee's head as she carefully and methodically wanted to explain what was happening.

"Ya know, Ms. G., back at the beginning of the semester when you first introduced the project. Remember? You kinda hinted at what it would be about, but you said you would tell us more as we got closer to the end. Well, I started thinking."

Raizel leaned forward, nodding her head in agreement and encouragement. She did not want to lose Shaynee's train of thought now by interrupting her with questions.

"Okay, go on…" was all Raizel uttered in a soft whisper.

Shaynee stared at the ceiling as though she was looking for the next words to magically fall out of the sky.

"I mean, look at me, Ms. G. What do you see?

"Huh? What do you mean, 'What do I see?' I see a beautiful, intelligent, curious young lady in front of me who is filled with passion and thirst for knowledge."

"Oh, gee, well thanks. That's very sweet of you. But, no, that's not what I mean at all. I mean look at my features.

My eyes, my hair, my skin tone. Ms. G., have you met my mom?"

"Of course, Shaynee. She came to our back-to-school night. She's a lovely woman."

"Not that part. Yeah, she's a good mom to me. And I love her. I really love her. But did you happen to notice that she's blonde? I mean a true blonde, a natural you know? Not bottle blonde like some of the other moms who have streaks or wanna-be-blonde like Reese Witherspoon.

"And her eyes. They're blue or what do you call them? Hazel. Like my brothers' eyes. And my dad? He's what, 6 foot something and I barely make five foot and nothing. Ms. G." Shaynee hesitated for what seemed forever. Finally, Shaynee blurted out, "I did it."

Raizel wasn't sure where this conversation was going. Well, yes, maybe, but in any event, she did not want to assume Shaynee was about to broach a topic that was very private, very personal, and very alarming. Uh, alarming to some people. But she had to ask. Shaynee was putting herself out there. And it was up to Raizel to take the bait.

"Okay, Shaynee, I give…what exactly did you do?"

"Ms. G., I took the test. I went ahead and bought an Ancestry kit right after you talked about this future project and how we needed to start thinking about what we wanted to do. It had to be something super important. This whole Ancestry thing has been on my mind. My entire family picture has been on my mind because I stand out in it. I don't fit in. There has to be a mistake somewhere and I had to find out. It's been on my mind, but I was too scared to go through with it.

"I mean I have always wondered why I look so different. I always wanted to ask my mom if I was adopted but she loved to tell me about the day I was born and wow, she was always so specific. Like she knew every step of the way when I was inside her and how I took so long to be delivered and what I looked like right away and all. So, I couldn't have been adopted, could I?"

Raizel was entering forbidden territory. It was not up to her to explore private family matters, but Shaynee was being very straightforward.

"Shaynee, have you asked your mom directly about this? I would think she would want to have this courageous conversation with you, don't you agree?"

"You see, Ms. G., here's the thing. I did the Ancestry test. I spit in the tube; I mailed it out. I set up my email to receive the data. And there it is. I got the data.

"And you know what? My mom's DNA definitely matches with me. I knew she had done the Ancestry years ago for fun, but I was too young, and I don't remember any part of it. She said she had done it as a joke or something because her sister gave her and my dad the kit as a Christmas gift, but she never shared the results with us.

"But wait, Ms. G., let me get to the real scary part. My dad? My dad, who I've known and loved all my life? His DNA isn't on there as a match. Nope. Nowhere. Nada. Not a spec, not one itty bitty chromosome. But there is someone I don't know on my list. This unknown person, this complete stranger to me has so many of those, what do they call them? I think it's cm's or something. That means this person is a direct link to me. So high up in the scale he could be a direct relative. No, not just a direct relative. He could be my father. So, tell me, Ms. G., what do I do now? How do I even present my project tomorrow? Tell me, please, I'm begging you because I'm really scared. I may have a father out there, a daddy who I never met who is my real biological daddy and I'm freaking out, Ms. G. I'm like really freaking!"

CHAPTER 10

Lila Libertino was smiling. Principal Libertino did not always get an opportunity to smile often, but Mama Lila, looking at her two children, Bessie and Benjamin, and her husband Darrius brought tears of joy to her eyes.

Winter break. No school for a few days, no student activities or sports she had to attend even though she thoroughly enjoyed all of them, and no sports or activities for her own children that she often sadly and guiltily missed. No husband away at conferences.

This was her dream. Surrounded by her family listening to their conversations, their passions, their frustrations, their gossip. She loved hearing their gossip because she did not have to deal with any of the drama. Plates clanging, forks and knives scraping, ice clinking, and all the while her two children were so busy talking and eating that the dinner time flew by. Almost.

"Mom," called Ben. "Mom, you're not listening to me. Hello, there, Mom."

Bessie chuckled, "C'mon, Benji, you know she's not ignoring you. She's just zoned out. Enjoying the ambiance of all of us."

"Really, Bess, why do you have to use such big words? Are you trying to impress me, 'cause you're not! You're just a punk."

Darrius joined in, "Hey, you two. Leave your mom alone. Can't you see she is in her secret happy place right now? It doesn't happen too often so leave her be. And Benjamin, if your sister wants to increase her vocabulary, she does not need to be judged by you. Do you hear me?"

Ben, his light hazel eyes stared at his glass recalcitrately, "Yes, sir."

Darrius smiled and leaned back in his chair, his large arms resting behind his head. He was satisfied that he had just solved a possible major explosion in the family unit.

Ben was not through, however, and he sat up in his seat and cleared his throat, shaking his head side to side as his soft curly black hair bounced up and down and he asked, "Uh, Dad, I have a serious question for you, and, well, for mom, too, I guess."

Darrius raised one eyebrow as he shot a questioning look at his son. He cocked his head to one side and with some hesitation broke the euphoric cloud that was floating around Lila.

"Lila, baby, I need your attention for a minute. Actually, we all do."

Lila, upon hearing her husband calling her, closed her eyes, bowed her head for a moment as if she were praying for peace, and whispered, "Sure, honey. What can I do for all of you tonight?"

"Well," Darrius continued, "it seems that our boy Benjamin has something he wants to discuss with us as a family. Are you up for this kind of discussion tonight? Perhaps another glass of that Pinot Grigio to help us along?"

Lila nodded. "Please, that sounds absolutely wonderful." Darrius leaned over and refilled her wine glass and gave Lila a knowing wink. "This won't take long, I don't think."

Ben coughed and Bessie, her long brown hair covering her eyes in true emo fashion, elbowed him in his side. "C'mon, bro, I want to chill tonight and play my Simms on my computer. I have a new basement to create."

Ben glared at his little sister. She was okay for a sister, but she was a bit nerdy and a brat and right now he needed her to be quiet and serious, a combination that she sorely lacked.

"Mom, Dad, there was a situation at school the other day and I kinda wanted your opinion on this. Ben's mesmerizing hazel eyes could cause a young teenage girl to catch her breath and his full upper lips were sporting a thin dark shadow of a soon-to-grow mustache. He was intelligent as much as he was handsome, and Lila knew she had to have 'the talk' with him about girls soon – if not yesterday.

"What's happening, son?" Lila asked soothingly, encouraging him to continue and not shake it off and go texting his friends what was on his mind.

"You know you can share anything with us," added

Darrius. He knew that some of these conversations with his son were too often like skating on thin ice and at any moment someone would sink below the surface or just give up and race away.

Ben faltered, took a deep breath, and started. He knew if he just kept on talking and didn't stop, he could get it all out and be done with what had been nagging him all week. Nagging him to the point where he couldn't concentrate on anything at school, not even that cute new girl with the tight soccer jersey in his science class, what was her name again?

"Okay, see it's like this. My math teacher, you know him, Mr. Pattree, well he was sent home the other day because some kid, I think he's a senior or something, this kid went up to the principal, Mr. English, and told him that Mr. Pattree was high on marijuana and he had proof because all you had to do was look at his eyes and that meant he was high because we had learned that in health class last year and so Mr. English called Mr. Pattree down to his office and sent him home and now we have some stupid substitute in who doesn't even know her math and all we are doing is these boring packets and I hate it but that's not what I want to talk about…"

"Take a breath, son," interrupted Lila. "And please stop using the word 'stupid' to describe another human being who is only trying to do her best for you and the other students."

"Mom, please!" begged Ben, "please let me finish before I am too scared to tell you the rest."

Bessie giggled when she heard Ben say he was scared, but Ben nudged her sharply and she cried out, "Ooomph."

Ben continued, "Mom, Dad, you always told me to do the right thing. I mean I know that's a Spike Lee mantra and all, but you want me to be brave and not let someone fall down a cliff just because he doesn't know how to defend himself, so I went to see Mr. English myself. And I told him that Mr. Pattree was not high but that he suffered from major allergies. And I knew that because I would hang out in Mr. Pattree's room during lunch so I could get extra help. And while I was with him, and a bunch of other kids as well, he would keep taking out his eye drops and his Zyrtec and complain about his allergies. He said it had something to do with the carpet in our room and he had asked to have the carpet removed but he was told that was impossible.

"He showed us the doctor's notes on his bottle, and it said to take two times a day for severe allergies and to use the eye drops to help take away the red stuff. Well, that's not really medical technical ya know, but damn it, oh God, I'm sorry I said that, but wow, he's such a good teacher and someone threw him under the bus just because he didn't like him."

Ben took a long, slow deep breath. "I heard that kid bad-mouthing Mr. Pattree because he failed his class and he said he was gonna get him back somehow. This has to be his way of doing it, don't you think?

"Anyway, I swore to Mr. English that I never saw Mr.

Pattree look or act high and you know what he said to me? You know what that bastard had the nerve to say?"

Darrius cleared his throat the minute he heard Ben say 'bastard' but he did not break Ben's speech.

"Mom, would you not believe a student who came to you and swore that their teacher was being wronged? I know you would. I know it. You're like that. Anyway, my principal questioned me. He asked me how would I know that Mr. Pattree was or was not high? Do you believe that? He was assuming I knew all about drugs and being high and that's not cool."

Ben was still talking, and his comments seemed to wander into all kinds of rabbit holes, but Lila's mind was suddenly somewhere else. She remembered that moment when a group of female students charged the secretaries in the main office and demanded to see her, and when they stormed into her room full of passion and out of breath from nerves, all they could breathlessly utter was how outstanding a teacher he was on and on, and, oh, no, did she commit the same lame excuse of not believing her students the same way that her son's principal had done?

More importantly, what had Lila done or not done to follow up with Carl? She thought the world of Carl, but at this exact moment where was he, what was he doing and how was his case proceeding? She suddenly had more to do this winter break than she realized.

CHAPTER 11

Lucas was squirming and moaning.

"Leave me alone, you bastard!"

"Oh, c'mon, son," whispered Angelo. *"It's okay. I love you. I love you so much, my boy, my son."*

"No," interrupted Walter. *"I love you, Lucas. Your mom and I love you, boy. We will do everything for you."*

"Lucas," uttered another voice. *Who was that talking to me? Who is that? Lucas could not make out the facial features, but he looked familiar.*

"Lucas," he repeated. *"It's me. It's Mr. DeWitt. I'm here for you, Lucas. I can't thank you enough for standing up for me. You are the real deal. You are a great student and an incredible athlete."*

"Don't listen to them, Lucas," hissed Angelo. *"They're telling you lies. It's all lies. You need to come with me. You need to leave your mother and that no good cop she married. How dare she marry that man. He's dangerous, Lucas. Stay away from him. Come with me, son. I'm the only one who can take care of you."*

Lucas was moaning and twitching but he could not open his eyes.

Walter put a strong hand on Lucas' shoulders. "Your mom and I love you, Lucas. We're gonna take care of you. You know that, don't you? We will see you through anything. Anything at all. Now stop struggling with me and let's go."

Carl DeWitt put his hand on Lucas's other shoulder. "I'll help you, too, Lucas. Me and your dad. Your new dad. He is the one who truly loves you. Stay away from that other man. He only wants to hurt you, Lucas. I know. I know that because my dad always hurt me. Listen to me."

Lucas wanted to scream. He wanted to run away. Something was holding him down and try as hard as he could he wasn't able to move.

"Lucas! Lucas!"

Who was calling him? Why couldn't he get up? His arms felt like heavy logs. He started kicking his legs. That's it. I can kick and start running. But, wait, someone grabbed his legs. Who was holding him down?

"Lucas, dude! Wake up, man! You are having one hell of a nightmare! Dude, bro, c'mon, wake the hell up!"

Lucas struggled. As hard as he could he moved his eyes and then moved them again until he slowly lifted his lids.

Max and Tommy were holding him down on the floor. And Jáquan was sitting on his legs.

"What are you guys doing?" yelled Lucas, still groggy and uneasy from such a disturbing nightmare.

The three boys sat back on their haunches. Tommy started, staring into Lucas's scrunched-up face, "Lucas, man, you were having an awful dream and you were thrashing your arms and legs all around and we didn't want you to get hurt.

"So Max and me, damn it, Lucas, we held you down by your shoulders and Jáquan grabbed your ankles. You kept shouting, 'Let me go, let me go, damn you!' but we were afraid for you."

Jáquan whistled, "Whew, like I ain't never seen anyone in the middle of a bad dream like that. You scared the shit outta me. Sorry."

Max reached over, put his arms under Lucas's shoulder, and hoisted him up to a sitting position. Lucas's sleeping bag was crumpled in a messy heap. "You woke us all up. Even Tommy's little brother got scared and ran out."

Lucas, sitting up now and taking some strong deep breaths looked around the room. There were Tommy's bunk beds where Tommy's little brother Sawyer slept on the bottom. Clothes were bunched up in various places on the floor. Shoved up against the wall were the sleeping bags of Max and Jáquan, squished and tossed as the boys had surrounded Lucas earlier.

"No kidding, man, you really scared us, Lucas," agreed Tommy. "You were thrashing all around and yelling but most of the time we couldn't understand what you were saying.

"Are you okay now? I mean, do you want to go home, or can you hang out longer with us? My mom's getting breakfast ready and then I thought we were going to play Madden. I got the latest version for Christmas."

Lucas nodded. He stared at the Tom Brady poster on the wall alongside a poster of Olivia Rodrigo. On the other side of the wall was a collection of Battle Royale posters. Lucas smiled knowing those were for Sawyer, who was nine.

Lucas liked Sawyer because every time Lucas would come to hang out Sawyer would get into a kneeling football stance and yell to Lucas, "C'mon, hotshot, try to get by me. I know you can't 'cause you're too slow. They call you Lazy Lucas and I know why! Hahahaha!" Lucas loved this teasing as he never had that kind of rapport with someone younger than him. He had no siblings and he secretly yearned for one, even a sister. He knew Sawyer looked up to him, and idolized him as Tommy would tell him. Tommy sounded a bit jealous about the admiration that was piled on Lucas, but he let it go.

The boys rolled up their sleeping bags in silence. They were deep in their thoughts and were afraid to discuss them. Tommy looked at his friends and decided to break the stillness that seemed to weigh them down. Guys did not want to get too emotional, but they were sincerely worried about Lucas. Ever since summer practices Lucas had not been the same. Hell, it all started a few years ago, but the boys were not that intuitive to observe that. But they knew Lucas was harboring something way too deep and maybe he would want to unburden himself. At least with his best guys.

"So, uh, Lucas. Uh…do you wanna share what your nightmare was about, man? I mean, you were actually having a rough time there for a while and it shook us up quite a bit. Even when we were holding you down 'cause we thought you were gonna hurt yourself…well, we are your best friends.…Bros for life, right? And we are here for you. You wanna talk about it…that is before we go downstairs 'cause Sawyer is a talker, man, and I can't trust him to keep his yap shut.

"And my mom, hell, the first thing she'll do is call your mom, and then who knows what else?"

Lucas tightened the cords on his rolled-up sleeping bag. He grabbed it and held onto it like it was his lifesaver. "I… uh…I'm going through some bad stuff, I guess. I get these dreams all the time and I know I'm supposed to tell my therapist. You know, the lady I have to see so I don't get sent to another school? Miss Anna is her name. She's cool. But, damn, she's a girl, I mean a grown-up girl and all…

"And I should probably tell her, but maybe I'll tell you guys first to see if I'm really going crazy or not."

Lucas stumbled at first, stopped and started and then he recounted the dream. Slowly at first, and then it seemed to pour out of him like a rushing stream. Lucas bit his nails every time he stopped to take a breath. This was a new habit of his and even Miss Anna noticed it. Lucas knew that because her eyes always dropped to focus on his hands to see if they were bleeding or something like that. He wasn't always sure. But he couldn't stop it. Not yet, anyway.

The guys knew his father had left town, but never really knew why. Lucas did not go into those specific details with them. Telling your guy friends that your father was sexually molesting you was not something he was ready to do. It was always going to be a struggle dealing with that trauma, and Miss Anna was helping, but he knew this pain would be with him forever. And the guys knew about Walter Young and his mom getting married and all. And they understood a guy would struggle to balance your biological father and your stepfather even if you never saw your real dad.

Jáquan was observing Lucas closely. He understood the difficulties of being an African American teenager, but he wasn't sure how he would deal with having a white stepfather. And Lucas, having a Black stepfather, well, he knew that was a challenge. Racial conversations did not always come easy with anyone let alone a bunch of teenagers. But their friendship was strong, and they believed in each other. Racial slurs, even jokingly, were off-limits and were never a part of their repertoire. Sports, girls, girls, and sports. Sex talks were frequent, too, but their accurate knowledge was extremely limited to hearsay and false bravado. Sometimes teachers who pissed them off for reasons they could not articulate, but that was the extent of their conversations for the most part.

"But then," Lucas continued, "I saw Mr. DeWitt in my dream. I mean, man, what happened to him? I think someone did him bad. I think a student might have been angry with him and said something to someone. But in my dream, he was there helping me. He was always trying to help me out."

Max, slowly twisting one of his tight afro strands with

one hand, jumped in, "You know, I heard it wasn't another student. I heard it was a teacher who made up a lie about Mr. DeWitt and got him fired. At least that's what I heard Mr. Tannereck say in math class before break. He was whispering to Officer Sheldrake, and they didn't think anyone could hear them. I thought I heard Officer Sheldrake mention Mrs. Winewrought, but I'm not a hundred percent sure."

Jáquan's pale green eyes opened wide. "You gotta be kidding me! That totally sucks. Can't we do something about this? We gotta be able to do something. Anything!"

Lucas picked up his sleeping bag and tucked it under his arm. He looked around the room at his best friends. "You know, you guys are the best. Waddya say we go grab that awesome breakfast Tommy's mom is making us and come up with a plan? I was thinking, well, just a thought… what if we started a petition when we get back to school? After all, it will shake some things up. We can start it, and I know if I call Riley she'll be right there helping us. She'll have it typed up with a million copies ready to be passed around. She is cool like that. Yeah?"

Jáquan scooped up his bag as did Max. They both nodded their heads in agreement along with Tommy who asked, "Riley? Really Lucas? Now you're hitting on Riley? You are one crazy dude, you know that?"

Lucas laughed and the boys were punching each other playfully as they raced out of the bedroom following the delicious wafting aroma of pancakes and bacon.

CHAPTER 12

"Livvy Shields?" hissed Beverly at the very attractive blonde woman standing in *her* kitchen using *her* spatula to make dinner for *her* husband. "Livvy Shields as in my husband's secretary? And, by the way, any relation to a Whitney Shields, one of my students?"

Livvy knew this was going to be awkward. She told Ted the day he asked her to move in with him. She knew that Beverly wasn't completely out of Ted's life. And to make matters worse, Livvy knew that her daughter was in Beverly's science class at school. How ironic was that?

Beverly, her small dark brown eyes simmering at Livvy, her voice fuming, "Well, aren't you the sneaky one moving into MY home the minute I'm not around? Won't your husband and daughter have something to say about this or are they completely unaware of your new sleeping arrangements?"

Ted, shoving his overgrown golden bangs out of his

bloodshot eyes, tried to intervene. He knew how difficult it was to interrupt Beverly when she was on one of her rants, but he attempted to anyway, "Beverly, please. You must understand…"

"Seriously, Ted? Understand? Does Livvy know the true Ted? The one who gets so incredibly angry when his dirty underwear isn't picked up from the floor or his dinner isn't ready when he walks in the door?

"Or, worse, how about the Ted who shoves you so hard you crash onto the floor, oh, and it was an accident of course."

Beverly turned her attention back to Livvy, "And do you want to see my numerous ER visits and write-ups or has Ted forgotten to mention those romantic moments?"

Livvy, her deep emerald, green eyes suddenly growing wide with fear, turned towards Ted and raised her shoulders as though questioning.

Ted was not to be outdone. He looked into Livvy's eyes which were brimming with tears, "I never, ever hurt Beverly. She is a drama queen from way back. She has fallen, yes, but not because of me. It's complicated, Livvy. Beverly is the ultimate klutz, tripping or falling all the time. I swear, Livvy. I swear on the grave of my dear mother, may she rest in peace."

"Oh, Ted," coaxed Beverly her raspy voice dripping with sweet venom, "let's not keep this raunchy romance in the dark. Really, sweetheart? You wanna go with that line? Okay." Beverly turned towards Livvy, and in one swift motion, drew her hand back and slapped Livvy on the face as hard as she could, the smack reverberating in the kitchen.

Livvy was thrown back a few steps, her eyes overflowing with the tears she tried to hold back as she sputtered, "Why, what..the hell?" She could not say another word she was so taken aback as one hand swiftly reached up to her reddened and swollen face and held it there touching the darkening hot wound.

A screeching and wickedly evil shrill sprang from Beverly. Her grating voice oozing with derision as she spit, "He's all yours, baby. I just wanted you to feel the pain I've felt all these years, and if you can live with that, then good riddance to both of you. I'm just gonna grab a few personal things and the two of you can live happily ever after.

"And, for the sake of your daughter, hell, I don't even like her so don't worry about me cozying in to tell her what a whore her mother is."

Livvy's eyes widened and with a newly found outrage and contempt, her overly large botoxed lips dripping spittle, she shouted, "Oh! You… bitch!"

Beverly smiled vindictively and snorted, "Oh, honey, you have no idea." And with that, she turned around, and ran up the stairs to her bedroom leaving Ted standing there with his hands stretched out utterly flummoxed over the entire incident. He never could handle Beverly.

He turned to Livvy and said, "I'm gonna make this up to you, baby. I swear it."

Livvy crumpled to the floor crying, looked up to Ted, and said, "You owe me big time, Ted. Oh, boy, you better believe it!"

Beverly stuffed two duffle bags and one large suitcase. She threw all her jewelry, perfumes, and hair accessories into a large gym bag. She didn't care if all of her things got tangled up or broken, she just wanted out of there as fast as she could.

She paused for a moment as she glanced at the large 18x24 wedding picture on the wall. Beverly sniffed back a sob. Beverly gazed at her picture seeing herself so young with dreamy eyes filled with hopes for their future together, smiling and so much in love. She spoke softly to the picture as though she were confessing a secret, "I'm not going to cry; I'm not going to break down. He hurt me. I thought we had something special. I thought we were a team. Well, I'm going to start over. I'm going to have a new life and it will not be with Ted. And any man who gets in my way will know I am no pushover. Not anymore. I am a new Beverly. Goodbye picture. Goodbye, dresser. Goodbye, closet. Goodbye, bed. Goodbye, room." Beverly chuckled at her childhood allusion to *Goodnight Moon*. She scooped up the bags and carefully plodded down the staircase.

She could hear Ted and Livvy in the kitchen. They were whispering. She did not care what they were talking about. She wanted no part of Ted. And to think, she was considering moving back in. What a joke. She was a joke.

Beverly picked up her overnight bag and her satchel she had dropped in the hallway. With her arms full, Beverly stepped outside and closed the door gently behind her for the last time. There was no going back. Not again. Not ever.

Beverly threw her belongings into the back seat of her car and slammed the door shut as though she were closing out her past. She turned around to glance at the house. The only home she ever owned where she thought she had found happiness and love. She whirled around and got into her car, turned it on, hit the sync control to listen to her favorite music, and sped off.

"Where am I going anyway?" she thought aloud. "Back to Alisa? I can't. I can't do that to her. She didn't buy into this bargain. I have no other choice. Mom? Looks like I'm coming home. Again."

And with new conviction, the music blaring, and with a familiar sinister smile on her face, Beverly drove into her future.

CHAPTER 13

Carl's eyes were closed. The gentle motion of the car was soothing and since he and Chip had not spoken one word since they left his father's house, he decided that completely shutting down was the easiest way to avoid any confrontation.

Before they left, Carl spoke to Lemont Jacobs, his union representative, briefly while Chip was cleaning out his car to make room for their journey.

"Uhhh, Carl," Lemont had started his conversation, "Remember, you are supposed to meet with a panel next week to review your situation. Telling them you cannot make it is not a good sign to them. They will think you're blowing them off.

"You're not blowing them off, are you, Carl?" Lemont's voice was getting louder, and his tone was on the edge of accusatory.

Carl was losing his patience. He had been suspended from his teaching position without ever finding out who had accused him, or on what grounds. Added to that horror he was feeling very depressed and was even considering, no, no, he was not going there again. Ever. That was not the way he wanted to handle his situation. He was going to see this to the very end because he knew he was a good person, a strong teacher, and a very decent human being.

Carl took a slow, deep breath before he answered Lemont. He chose his words carefully and spoke slowly as though he was thinking of each word before he uttered them. "Lemont, I know you are doing your job, and I appreciate all your support. I want to go to this meeting. I need to go to this meeting. Unfortunately, my mother just suffered a heart attack. She is asking for me. My brother is going to take me to see her, but, Lemont, she lives in another state. It's going to be a few days before I can get back.

"What would you do, Lemont? Would you go see your mother in case she doesn't make it more than a few days, or would you ignore a dying woman's plea and attend the panel that is going to decide whether or not you have a job? A future. Tough call? I don't think so, Lemont. I don't think so at all. I can always find a job, but I sure as hell cannot find another mother. You get me?"

There was silence on the other end of the call. Carl knew Lemont was formulating a response.

"Carl?" Lemont's voice was suddenly taking on a more compassionate tone. "Man, I am so sorry. Look, you take your time. Go be with your mom. Stay as long as you need to. I will talk to the higher-ups and make sure they know you are not avoiding them, not playing some stupid little game of waiting them out.

"But if it's okay with you, would you check in with me on a daily basis? I need to know what your situation is and sometimes I am collecting information that is important to share with you."

Carl let out a long sigh. He had not realized he had been holding his breath that entire time Lemont was talking.

"Lemont, I can't thank you enough. And by the way, before I forget, did you get those reference letters I sent you? I can get more if you need them. Just tell me. I will do whatever I can to make this right again. I need to do that for me. I need to do that for everyone else whose heart is being ripped out like mine. We good now?"

Lemont closed his eyes, a small tear slipping down one side of his unshaven cheek. He hated feeling this way, feeling so helpless with a client he knew deep in his gut was being wronged. He wanted a good outcome for Carl. He wanted Carl to be allowed to return to his classroom and continue working with students and making a difference. There were others who he knew were evil and had done despicable things and they certainly deserved their consequences. Lemont may have attempted to help those few individuals, but in the end, they were let go with prejudice as their final letters stated. They would never work in education again.

But it was different with Carl. He had read the letters

that Carl had sent him to be used as good solid references. Those letters that he read were the most heartwarming praises for a teacher. They were sincere, positive, and absolutely glowing. Something was inherently wrong in this system when lies and insinuations twisted someone up so tightly that it broke them. He did not want Carl to reach that point. So he wiped his eyes, cleared his throat, and answered, "Yeah, Carl. We are good, man. Now go see your mom. I'll be saying a prayer for her tonight, too." With that, Lemont clicked off.

Carl smiled to himself. He opened his eyes and turned to look at Chip. Chip was focused on his driving and did not acknowledge that Carl was staring at him or maybe he was just ignoring him. He couldn't tell for sure, but it was uncomfortable.

Finally, Chip took a deep breath, rubbed his eyes, and said softly, "Man, Carl, were you actually…I mean…back at the house…did you…would you have…?"

Carl interrupted him. It was too painful to hear Chip struggle to complete a sentence. "Chip, I know we have not been very close. Hell, we have never been close. And so, things have happened to me in the last few months, and well, I have not had anyone I could turn to. No one. Not a best friend, a brother, a girlfriend, nobody, nada.

"My life suddenly went down the shitter so to speak. And I couldn't see tomorrow or the next day or the next month let alone next year. Since I happened to check on the house like I always do, I had a thought. It was a dark thought. I held that gun in my hand and I thought for a second, really less than a second – should I end it? Could I end it?"

Chip's lips were quivering. He was squeezing the wheel of the car so tightly his knuckles had turned a ghostly shade of white. He sniffed hard but would not look at Carl. He was afraid to see the look of desperation in his older brother.

Carl continued, "And then I thought of Emma. Had Emma talked to me about her situation, maybe, just maybe I could have helped her or at least had her speak with someone who could have convinced her that she had a future, a good life ahead of her if only she could get past that nightmare she was living in.

"And then I realized I was talking about *me*. It was my nightmare, and did I have a future, and more importantly, could I get past my own darkness? And as I sat there, I knew that I had done nothing wrong. I was… I *am* a good person, a good educator and I will be damned if I allow another human being to decide my future, my potential for me. I am going to fight this, Chip and right before you well, barged into the house, I had already decided that I was not going to end my life, but rather I was going to go into hell with a blaze of glory kicking and screaming about my innocence."

Chip turned his head slightly and looked long and hard at his brother. Chip wiped his eyes with the back of his hand and smiled. "Damn, Carl, I thought you were gonna shoot the shit outta me for dissing you all our lives."

Suddenly, Carl snorted and that became a chuckle and then he burst out laughing so hard his stomach cramped. Chip's eyes widened in disbelief and then he joined his brother as the two of them howled and giggled as if they were both little boys again giggling at some silly television show.

And together they drove to see their mother – brothers in a newfound bond.

CHAPTER 14

Cindy sat in the oncologist's office nervously reading the latest copy of *People*. She wasn't reading it earnestly, more like flipping through the pages to keep herself from crying.

Mattie, her mother, was meeting with the latest in a string of medical professionals who would go over her recent diagnosis of breast cancer and the treatment she was about to undertake. Cindy was deep in thought. *So this is how I'm going to spend my school break this year. Staying at home close to mom and taking care of her, the house, the shopping, the cleaning. Damn it all to hell.*

And then as quickly as Cindy was streaming those feelings in her head, she started shaking her head from side to side vigorously as if she could excise those negative thoughts. *I'm lucky I have a mom who loves me and takes such good care of me. I'm being selfish. I'm being immature.* Cindy sighed audibly causing the desk receptionist to look up from her computer.

"Are you okay, honey?" she drawled, her southern accent dripping with sugary sweetness.

Cindy looked up to see an elderly woman staring, her red nail-polished hands still curled on the keyboard, smudged bifocal glasses hanging on the very tip of her rather large nose, and a wad of gum poised to pop a sloppy bubble.

Cindy gulped. She did not mean to draw attention to herself. Especially in a doctor's office. Cindy cleared her throat and said, "I'm okay, thank you. Sorry if I disturbed you."

The receptionist wasn't buying Cindy's response. "I'll tell you what, sweetie, why don't I bring you on back so you can be with your mom while she talks with the doctor? Is that alright? Are you okay with going back there? I mean, they're just talking and all right now so it's nothing you have to worry about, you know what I mean?"

Cindy had not planned on sitting in with her mother while the doctor was explaining those things, the scary, ugly cancer things. Cindy was uncomfortable enough as it was, and she wasn't sure she wanted to hear the details. It only made the matter that much more real. Reality was not what Cindy wanted. She was too young for this. She wanted to be home playing games on her computer or watching the latest season of *Stranger Things* while eating popcorn.

But she had to be strong. Miss Anna, her therapist, had been working with her on how to handle this new development about her mom, but Miss Anna was gone during the break. She was getting married and going to Aruba for her honeymoon, wherever that was so she couldn't contact her till after she was back in school.

One of the biggest exercises Miss Anna had practiced with her was how to respond to the hard facts of her mother's cancer. Cindy struggled with this; most of the time she ended up crying even when she was sitting in Miss Anna's office. Cindy hated coming out of her therapist's office, her eyes swollen, and having to pretend she was just fine when her mother picked her up.

But she wasn't fine. None of this was fine. These were the times when she prayed to God at night that she already had her share of her life being unfair. And now this? When would she get a break? When would her life shine a little happiness on her instead of gloom and doom?

Cindy sat up. Enough of this negativity. She looked at the receptionist's desk trying to find her name plate so she could be more respectful when she answered her. Teetering on the edge of the desk, Cindy saw a tarnished silver plate with the name Lilybeth Armstrong.

"Ms. Armstrong?" Cindy spoke so softly Lilybeth had to lean forward to hear her.

"Yes, punkin?"

"Could I go back and sit with my mom?"

Lilybeth smiled, her one front tooth so badly chipped she looked like she had been in a fight. "C'mon, honey girl, I'll take you back there. Now don't you worry about their talk, cause some of it might not make sense to you right now, but in time, it will. It surely will."

Cindy followed Lilybeth slowly as they shuffled through the maze of halls and doorways and mini offices. Cindy felt as though she should have dropped Skittles as she wandered past so many openings and secret vestibules. She glanced furtively at each one afraid someone from Harry Potter would materialize and whisk her far away to another land, almost wishing that would happen so she would not have to accept the reality that was about to slip over her like an unwanted shroud changing her life forever.

Finally, Lilybeth stopped at a closed door with a small gold plaque hanging in the middle that read:

> Not everything that is faced can be changed, but Nothing can be changed until it is faced.
> James Baldwin

Lilybeth knocked gently and when she heard the familiar, "Come" she opened the door, ushered Cindy in, and closed the door gently after leaving Cindy standing in a large office. Cindy's eyes bulged wide open at seeing her mother sitting in a dark brown leather chair, her shoulders hunched over and her hands in her face.

Cindy stared at her mother for just a second and then whipped her face to the elderly doctor sitting behind a desk the size of Montana. Cindy, always an introvert, for one brief moment, lost all her inhibitions.

"What did you say to my mother?" Cindy shrieked painfully.

CHAPTER 15

Beverly drove her car without paying attention to road signs or speed limits. She was on muscle memory as much as she wished these memories were completely and thoroughly eradicated from her brain.

It would take her forty-five minutes to reach the outskirts of her childhood neighborhood. That meant it was going to take her a good solid hour in the morning to get to work and possibly an hour and a half to drive back to her old home. Beverly was already swallowing hard with the knowledge that she was taking a major step backward by returning home.

She didn't want to remember, but the nightmares came flooding into her brain and she did not have a lifesaver to hoist her out of the darkness that enveloped her, drowning her in the hell she thought she had escaped from years ago.

Beverly had slipped into her house carefully opening and then locking the door without making a sound. It was late that night. It was only 11:30 but her father would be livid. And just as she entered the hallway there he was standing in his old boxer shorts and his sleeveless white undershirt, a large glass vase in one hand and a bat in the other.

"Dad? What the hell?"

"What do you mean coming in this house so damn late, young lady? Here I thought you were some kind of goddamned burglar trying to steal my things. But I was ready for you. Oh, yeah, I was ready and I would have beat the living shit out of you if you were anybody else!"

"Dad, c'mon….put that vase and baseball bat down. Now!"

Suddenly Jack Stevenson hurled the large vase against the wall shattering it in a million pieces. Some of the pieces ricocheted off the wall and pierced the arms of Beverly's sleeveless dress where they clung to her skin embedded like a glass tattoo.

The blood spurted out through the penetrated slits of her skin, sluiced down over her clenched knuckles and fingers, and dripped onto the floor. Between the sounds of exploding glass and the warm rivulets of blood rolling down her arm, Beverly screamed in horror and crumpled in a bloodied heap onto the floor.

Beverly's mother, Darlene, a small brown-haired mousey woman whose head was layered in bright pink sponge curlers came racing around the corner and stopped just before stepping onto the multitude of broken glass on the hardwood floors.

"Jack Stevenson! What in God's tarnation are you doing to that poor child? You knew she was coming in late, and you went and tried to scare the bejesus out of her! What's got into you?"

Jack looked at his wife with the same beady dark eyes as Beverly's and spit out, "Cause that girl has got to learn some manners around here. She's out with who knows who doing who knows what and I ain't gonna allow this to happen here. She's letting them boys touch her vajayjay this late at night and I ain't gonna let her live here no more. She's become a slut, a whore and she needs to leave!"

Beverly looked up at her father and gathered up all the nerve her 19-year-old self could muster and with bitterness seeping from her lips cried, "I'm tired of you saying lies about me. Tired of you thinking I'm doing something I'm not. You can't beat me anymore. You can't throw things at me anymore and if I want to be with a boy, well, I'll be damned, I'm going to go out with whoever the hell I want to."

Darlene started shaking. These fights were becoming more and more frequent, and it caused her stomach to tie up in knots and her heart to pound faster and faster as though it would come bursting out of her. She had never stood up to Jack. She was taught to obey her husband no matter what and while she disagreed when he slapped Beverly or spanked her bottom as a child, she never stopped him; she just picked up the pieces of broken things whether it was Beverly or vases or whatever else Jack would try to destroy to show his false elevated place in the world. He was the king; he was the boss, and no one was going to tell him otherwise, that is of course unless it was at his place of work where he was the lowest of the low in the assembly line.

Darlene knew that Jack's father had beaten him. Regularly. And oftentimes for no reason at all other than the fact that Jack was the only one in the living room or sitting at the kitchen table. It didn't matter. Jack's father was so tormented, so distraught that he never could see his own wrongdoings. And so he took it out on Jack. Jack's mother left them when Jack was only ten. She took his baby sister with her and he never saw either one of them again. Ever.

Was this cause enough for Jack to be so hard on Beverly? Was he punishing her for his own demons? It was not fair and Darlene had put up with his faults for too long.

She walked behind Jack gently swiping at the broken shards on the floor and crouched down next to her sobbing daughter. She peered up at her husband who stood over the two of them, his fist squeezed tight and shaking, his other hand still clenching the baseball bat, his eyes open but seeing a vision far away. Darlene felt her heart tighten, and her stomach heave. She desperately gulped the air for courage and then she roared, "Jack, leave this room. Now! Go! Pack your bags, walk out of this house, and don't ever come back. I won't tolerate you one second more! Do you hear me? Because if you are not out of this house by the time I take care of my bleeding and frightened daughter I will call the police. Do you hear me?" Darlene could not stop shaking, whether it was from fear or her newly formed bravery she was not sure.

Jack, still holding the baseball bat in his left hand looked at Darlene and started swinging the bat while cautiously shuffling towards her.

"Don't you come one step closer to us, you son of a bitch. I've listened to you for 25 years and I am done. Go on. Come closer and see this piece of glass I just picked up?"

The large glass fragment shimmered with various hues of red, gold, and blues from the reflection of the hall light, but all Jack saw was the sharp sliver of ice that signaled pain, and he stopped. He dropped the baseball bat on the floor and turned around towards the bedroom, but before he turned the corner in the hallway he stopped and shouted in a heartless voice filled with hatred and disgust, "I'll leave, woman! But I won't be held responsible for her anymore. She's all yours and good riddance to the both of you!"

That was the last time Beverly had seen her father. He dropped dead from a massive heart attack last July while mowing the lawn. Even though they no longer lived together, Jack would come back to take care of the yard. The only good thing that ever came out of that marriage was the large life insurance Jack had purchased. That allowed Darlene to pay off her mortgage and live in peace from then on.

Beverly slowed down as she approached the house. She had not realized that her flashback had her hands shaking on the steering wheel and her entire body had broken out in a cold sweat.

She grabbed her water bottle, swallowed the rest of the cool liquid, and wiped her forehead with her sleeve.

She pulled her car into the driveway and took a deep breath. She had to think of the exact words she wanted to say to her mother because she did not want to rehash the past few weeks right now. She needed to rest and recuperate and forget about Ted. Forget about his new girlfriend Livvy. Forget about the drama at school. And most importantly, forget about Carl, wherever the hell he was.

CHAPTER 16

Barbara Atkinson was sitting alone in her office, her Spotify turned softly on to the complete hit songs of the 70s in the background. This was her time; her alone time and she craved the solitude. She loved catching up on her paperwork without the daily irritating interruptions that constantly had her brain fried by the end of the day. At this rate she knew she would catch up on her emails, her teacher observations, and most importantly, clean her office of numerous stacks of stuff she liked to hide in a folder labeled FATS for File All This Shit.

Barbara knew that in order for her to function she needed to be in a mindset of complete and total concentration, especially when it came to paying attention to details. The ability to focus was never easy for her but she learned how to compensate and hiding out in her office during winter break was her best solution. No one was in the building save a few of the custodial staff who were busy completing some deep floor cleaning and waxing knowing there would not be the stampede of hundreds of dirty feet trampling on their work.

There was a knock on her door just as Barbara opened her first email. *"Damn it!"* she said out loud knowing that no one would hear her.

"Come in," she called out gruffly as her good mood was suddenly heading south in a hurricane hurry.

The door opened slowly as if the intruder had heard her loud negative remarks regarding the knocking and feared coming in too quickly. Ryan Netsworth, his skinny oval glasses fogging at the edges from his heavy breathing tip toed in as though walking on glass. He was in his late 40s, extremely slim to the point of looking emaciated, his faded yellow thinning hair falling in strands over his gray eyebrows.

Barbara looked up from her computer, her shoulders sagging with recognition of the unwanted guest. She stood up and trudged slowly around her desk. "Good day, Mr. Netsworth," her voice aloof and condescending. "How can I help you today, sir?"

"Well, Ma'am," Ryan began slowly, choosing his words carefully as he was painfully aware that he was interrupting the administrator. "I have orders from Dr. Libertino to install a camera in the building. I'm sorry to bother you, but I just want to check and make sure I'm in the right corner of the school. Seems like it's way down the hall somewheres and I got to figure out the logistics you see.

"I was hoping you wouldn't mind walking me down to the actual spot Dr. Libertino wants the new camera cause it's gonna take me some time to hook up the lines and all."

Barbara sighed. An interruption to her plans. She muttered softly, "The best laid plans and stuff…" She turned around and trudged over to her desk, scooped up her keys, twisted around to face Mr. Netsworth, and forced a smile.

"Okay, Mr. Netsworth, follow me, please."

Barbara signaled for Ryan to exit her office, then she followed, closing her door, and making sure it was locked. Then they both headed down the long, quiet hall.

Barbara felt a slight twinge of guilt thinking about the way she treated Mr. Netsworth. He was, after all, only doing his job. She had completely forgotten that Lila, knowing Barbara would be in the office for a few days during the break, had asked her to show Ryan exactly where she wanted the new camera installed. Lila was tired of that one dark hallway where students hid during the school day. She couldn't have security constantly supervising one small section of her large building, but if she was able to install a camera there, well, then she would have a bit more control over the situation.

Barbara reluctantly attempted to engage in a conversation that was polite without being too personal. "So, Mr. Netsworth, how is your break going?"

Mr. Netsworth chuckled, "Well, you know, Ma'am…"

Barbara interrupted him, "Please call me Barbara or Ms. Atkinson, whichever is more comfortable for you."

Ryan cleared his throat, "Sorry, Ms. Atkinson. You see, it might be break time for the kids, but maintenance doesn't ever get time off. This is our best opportunity to come out to the schools and do some installations and repairs while the buildings are empty. Hah, and quiet." Ryan laughed at his own attempt at a joke.

Barbara cackled, trying to be more sociable. "I know what you mean, sir. That is exactly why I'm here by myself.

"Here, let's turn this corner right over there, and let me show you where Dr. Libertino wants the camera installed."

It took Barbara about ten minutes to explain to Mr. Netsworth exactly what Lila wanted to be built in that dark corner. Barbara remembered only too well the incident earlier in the year with Lucas and Jilly. In addition to those two getting caught in a very inappropriate situation, she had to suspend a few other students for sneaking into that corner and munching on some edibles that another student had brought into the building and was selling for a nice profit. Oh, uhh, what did that young entrepreneur call it again? Oh, yeah, chocolate surprise for only five dollars a square.

With Mr. Netsworth well on his way to placing the hall camera in the perfect setting, Barbara felt comfortable enough to leave him on his recognizance.

Walking through the halls, Barbara felt a close kinship with the building. She knew it wasn't *her* building, but as often as Barbara lived there day in and day out, she knew the connection was more than just a feeling.

And just as Barbara's face cracked open a smile that was too long in the making, and with a little pep in her step as she turned the corner, she came face to face with Alisa Saper.

"Ummphhh!" Alisa's head was face down reading her cell phone and did not hear another person rounding the corner when she smacked right into, of all people, Barbara Atkinson.

"Excuse me, Miss Saper!" Barbara bellowed, wiping her nose from bumping into Alisa's forehead. "What on earth possessed you to be in the building over break? And did you inform security that you would be here? Why, the cameras alone might have signaled for an intruder and sent the police here!"

"I am so sorry, Ms. Atkinson. Why, to be truthful, the reason I am here today is because I need to see you. I must see you. It's extremely important and when I called the office, and no one was answering, I was hoping maybe you were here, and well, I took a chance to come into the building in hopes that you were here and when I drove into the parking lot and saw your car, and yes, I remembered which car was yours, I was thinking that just maybe you might have a few minutes to spare to talk to me and, oh, God, I know I am rambling, but I really am nervous right now and I just gotta talk to you."

Alisa stopped talking for a moment, and took a breath, her shoulders shaking from nerves and her left eye twitching a bit.

Barbara stood there, puzzled. What on earth is going on around here, she thought to herself. This poor child!

"Alisa, come with me to my office. Let's sit down, relax and you can tell me everything that's on your mind."

And with that, the two women walked down the hall and disappeared around another corner.

CHAPTER 17

Neva curled up on her couch, her softest throw covering her legs keeping her warm and toasty as the cold winter winds howled outside. She had one hand resting on Atticus, her golden retriever, and one hand holding the latest Nora Roberts novel she was looking forward to reading. But Neva had yet to open the book. She stared at the cover for what seemed like hours. Finally, Neva sat up, placed the book on the table next to her, and reached for the phone.

Neva knew she was not allowed to contact Carl, but she would willingly be damned to hell if she did not try to see how her favorite colleague and special friend was doing. It had been, what…over two months since he was sent home.

"This is utterly ridiculous," Neva said out loud. Atticus looked up at his master, cocked his one ear, and whimpered. Neva smiled at her beloved furry companion and cooed, "It's okay, my Atticus, love. I'm just upset with myself for not doing something I should have done a long time ago.

"I hate always following the rules. Sometimes it just doesn't make any sense and, in this case, dear Atticus, I am 100% right. I must do something, and I mean right now."

And with that, Neva clicked on her texting app on her phone and scrolled down to find Carl's name. She sat there staring at her blank screen waiting for … inspiration… a calling from above giving her the okay sign…or maybe just a dose of courage. Neva took a deep breath and began her message:

Carl, I am sorry this message has taken so long for me to send. I want…no, I need to know you are okay. Is there anything I can do for you? Is there anyone I can talk to? I don't even know what to talk about since I, well, everyone is really in the dark as to why you are not in school.

I guess you cannot tell me the reason or reasons why you were sent home, but I can assure you that you have my back. I miss you. Your students miss you. And (LOL) Atticus misses you, too 😊 .

Dearest Carl, please let me know you are doing well and if there is anything, and I do mean anything, do not hesitate to contact me. I know you are probably not allowed to talk to me, at least that's what I'm thinking since you haven't come by to see me or call or even text. But I'll be damned if I am going to leave you out in the cold to hang.

Send me something…a smoke signal, a secret postcard, something!

Missing you terribly and worried sick.

Your partner, Neva

Neva hit the send button quickly before she lost any semblance of the potential consequences of her actions. She didn't care anymore. She put the phone back on her end table, bent down, grabbed Atticus by his ears, and kissed him right on his cold nose.

"Thank you, Atticus, my brave soldier. And just for giving me that extra ounce of bravery, I am going to reward you with a treat and me with some Downtown Abby tea I bought at the mall yesterday! Oh, yeah!"

Neva got off the couch and scurried into her kitchen with Atticus, wagging his tail ferociously in tow.

• • •

Lila Libertino sat alone at her kitchen table, her second cup of coffee growing cold, her scrambled eggs and toast still untouched. Both her children were squirreled in their rooms either playing video games, texting, or plotting the next major gift they wanted for Christmas. Even Darrius had excused himself after breakfast and was out in the garage, his unique man cave, banging on pieces of wood in hopes of creating the next best frame for the family picture.

The conversation she had with her son the other night at dinner was still weighing heavily on her heart. Ben's exact words were plaguing her, ringing in her ears over and over again: *he's such a good teacher and someone threw him under the bus just because he didn't like him.*

Her son had approached his school principal in order to defend a teacher he felt was wronged. Benjamin. My son, who would rather play basketball all day at the park than come home for dinner. When had he grown up so much? When had he developed such a strong sense of right and wrong that he was willing to place himself in such a precarious situation as to question the highest authority in the building? She smiled. Maybe we have done something right here as parents she thought to herself.

Lila shook her head from side to side as if she were trying to shake that conversation out of her mind. And then just as quickly as her self-bragging about herself as a super parent, another image popped into her head. No, it didn't pop. It exploded inside of her. Three girls, three very brave and angry girls had blown passed her secretary and stormed into her office to demand to know why their favorite teacher was tossed out of the building.

They were all talking so quickly, so emotionally, so dramatically it was hard to slow them down let alone find a single thread that made sense. There were tears and smiles and lots of raised voices not to mention a major raid on her candy dish!

But in the end, when she finally calmed the girls down and rendered poor Amelia free of any guilt for allowing the girls to give her the slip, Lila, her eyes wet with pride at the girls' fearlessness, was able to convince the girls that something would be done.

"The most important thing you can do right now, girls," Lila had said encouragingly, "is to sit down and write everything you just said to me in a letter. I will then deliver that letter personally to ensure that it goes into the appropriate hands. After that, we will have to rely on the hope that the truth comes out and Mr. DeWitt is exonerated of any wrongdoing and returns to us as soon as possible."

And with that suggestion, plus some paper, pens, and the rest of the candy from her special bowl, Riley, Jilly, and Cindy went to work writing as vigorously as three teenage girls could write.

Lila went back to her desk, blew her nose, opened her computer, and composed a short email to Lemont Jacobs.

Lila took a sip of her cold coffee. It was time. If three freshmen girls and her son were going to brave authority, then it was high time she did the same. She grabbed her cell phone, left the cold coffee and her uneaten breakfast on the table, and headed to her office. She needed to be in her personal sanctuary when it came to dealing with such serious issues.

Lila closed the door to her home office. Her family

knew that when that door was closed Lila was off-limits to everyone. Something was happening in that office and no one, not even her mother resting in heaven, was allowed to interrupt her.

Lila sat at her desk and stared at her phone. She knew the longer it took to call up the number the stronger the odds of her procrastinating. *Suck it up, woman, and do the right thing like Ben and Spike Lee say!* And with that, she scrolled down her contact list to her superintendent and pressed the call button.

CHAPTER 19

Mattie looked up to see her daughter enter the office very slowly. She was surprised to see Cindy come in at all. Mattie had left her daughter in the receptionist's lounge knowing that hearing her oncologist discuss the nitty gritty details of her breast cancer would be too much for Cindy.

Cindy staggered in, hesitating at first, and then seeing her mother with her head in her hands, she shrieked, "What did you say to my mother?"

Cindy did not wait for a response. With her newfound courage, she hurled herself into her mother's arms and squeezed her tightly as if her body was physically capable of infusing her mother with all the love and medicine that would make her well again.

"Mom," whispered Cindy, "I'm here. And I'm going to be here with you every step of the way. Now, let's find out what's happening to you and together we will be stronger. I know it."

Mattie's eyes filled with tears, and she let them fall unabashedly.

Dr. Paul Noonent smiled. It wasn't often that he witnessed a scene such as this in his office. At 52 years old he had viewed many scenarios from anger and hatred to jealousy and sorrow but seeing the love and support from this teenage daughter gave Dr. Noonent hope and inspiration for the youth of today.

He knew he had to deliver the information not only for Mattie but for her daughter as well and he also knew that processing this much data, this much clinical terminology was overwhelming and frightening.

"Cindy?" he began, his pale blue eyes twinkling and his toothy grin wide showing a beautiful collection of pearly whites, "your mom has told me a great deal about you. Especially the part where she says how much you are a help to her and how independent you have become recently.

"That's very good to know, because, honestly, Cindy, this is going to be a long, arduous journey for the both of you. Do you know what arduous means, honey?"

Cindy nodded up and down furiously. "Uhhh, yeah, I think it means like hard, right?"

Dr. Noonent smiled. "You are absolutely right there. So let's begin, shall we? There is much information to learn about what your mom has and to start with we need to give it a name. Yes, it is breast cancer, but it is specifically called Triple-Negative Breast Cancer."

Cindy did not want to interrupt, but her face suddenly

scrunched up into a knot and Dr. Noonent knew how to interpret those signs immediately.

"Yes, Cindy? You want to know why it's called Triple-Negative and not just plain old damn breast cancer, right?"

Cindy's eyes widened. How did you know that?"

Dr. Noonent laughed easily, his portly frame jiggling underneath his lab coat. "Because everyone I know is confused by this label. It doesn't make sense at first, but it will soon, I promise."

And so, Dr. Noonent continued explaining about a lumpectomy versus a mastectomy followed by radiation and chemotherapy. When he started to talk about nausea and hair loss, Cindy lost it. She turned to her mom and grabbed her arm.

"Oh, God, Mom, I'm so sorry. I want to help you. I want to make this all go away and I….and I….."

Mattie twisted her body around and took Cindy by both shoulders. "Look, baby, it's going to be okay. Dr. Noonent has explained all the ramifications of this horrible disease and with you by my side, well, together we're going to kick the shit out of this cancer. You hear me?! Now, no more tears, no more apologies ….no….no…baby. Remember we have the best doctor here and he is going to take this journey with us. He is going to make me whole again. Isn't that right, Dr. Noonent? Please tell my daughter I am right!"

Dr. Noonent looked at his patient and then at her daughter. This was the hardest part of his job. He did not want to be pessimistic. He did not want to spread doom and gloom. He needed his patient to be as positive as she possibly could.

"Mrs. Newport…. and Cindy, I am going to do everything humanly possible to make sure we kick this cancer right in the, excuse me, in the ass, and get you back to living a full and happy life. But I also need you to start making some major changes in your life regarding how well you take care of yourself and together, hell, together we can conquer everything.

"Now I have some more handouts to give to you, the name of a counselor I want you to see, and in reality the both of you should go see the counselor so you can hear the information together and share your feelings at the same time. I want you to start setting up your next appointments. Any other questions for me at this time?"

Mattie and Cindy both nodded no at the same time. Mattie stood up and reached out her hand to her doctor. Dr. Noonent pushed back his leather chair, came around from his desk, and instead of shaking her hand, he wrapped his large arms around Mattie and gave her a reassuring hug.

"Together, okay?" he said encouragingly.

"Thank you," Mattie uttered, her voice swallowed by her emotions.

Cindy took Mattie's hand in hers and together they left the office.

CHAPTER 20

Starbucks. Noon. Winter break. Jilly looked around at her friends. They were all here: Cindy, Tommy, Shaynee, Mateo, Whitney, Piper, Linette, Jáquan, Max, and Sofia. They had even called on Junay to be a part of this group. And Riley. And, yes, Lucas.

Cindy looked a bit frazzled, but she wouldn't explain why. Riley would probably find out later when Cindy would eventually tell her. Shaynee wanted to tell everyone something, but she was holding back, her lips pressed tightly together to help her from spilling whatever she was hiding. And Linette, hmmmmm. Something was definitely up with Linette. She looked different, but Jilly couldn't quite figure it out. Whitney was busy on her cell phone texting somebody, probably everybody. Junay had her nose in her new Driver's License Manual. Tommy kept poking at Lucas who chewed on his straw while staring at the floor. Sofia and Max were holding hands. Oooh, new couple. Piper was wearing her soccer uniform and was constantly checking her new iPhone since she was waiting to get picked up for her game. Mateo sat quietly munching on his muffin, his eyes glued on Riley. Finally, Jilly looked at Riley and nodded the go-ahead.

Riley stood up; her favorite caramel crunch Frappuccino almost completely sucked down to the bottom. Riley tended to eat hard candy or drink something very quickly when she was nervous. This wasn't her group; these weren't her people. Other than Jilly and most recently Cindy, she did not have people. She looked around the group, each one with a drink in their hands along with a muffin or a bagel that everyone was taking a bite out of and then passing the treats around.

Their Starbucks had become their hangout. They were too young to drive to the mall, they were too old to go hang out at the playground and there were too many of them to converge in someone's home. So, Starbucks it was, and they were very comfortable lounging in the couches and the old heavily cushioned reading chairs with thick bulging armrests.

Riley began, haltingly at first, and then her courage grew, and she spoke louder and faster and more authoritatively as if she were running for class office.

"Okay. Hey. Alright." Riley wasn't sure how to begin.

Tommy laughed out loud. "Hey, c'mon, Riley. Waddya got for us? Huh? How come we were all summoned here?"

Lucas snortled under his breath. "Yeah, Maddog, what's up with the 'hey, I need all of you to meet at Starbucks, like now.' Was there some kind of code in there?"

Riley choked down the rest of her Frappuccino and looked at each one of them in the eyes, slowly, cautiously. They were all staring up at her as if she had the answers to their life's problems.

She knew she had better begin or they would soon all just get up and disperse out to another hangout – TJ Maxx or Dick's or someone's basement.

"Okay, I'm ready. I'm ready. Chill for a second here while I try to say what's on my mind.

"So you all know that a couple of months ago, Mr. DeWitt was taken out of the building…"

Suddenly, everyone in the group stopped fidgeting, texting, or eating. All eyes were on Riley. Riley took a deep, gentle breath and was about to continue.

"Hey, yeah, like what's that all about because…" interrupted Max who had taken his hand out of Sofia's hand to raise it high in the air.

"Max," admonished Riley, "This isn't the classroom. Don't raise your hand and don't interrupt me till I'm done."

Max dropped his hand and Sofia quietly took it and gently placed it back in her clutches.

Riley started again. "So, right before break started, Jilly, Cindy, and I went to see Dr. Libertino. We decided we needed to say something, anything, in defense of Mr. DeWitt."

Riley looked at Cindy and Jilly who were both nodding their heads in agreement. Cindy was blowing her nose which seemed unusually red as though she had been crying before arriving at Starbucks. But then again, Riley always found Cindy crying somewhere and decided not to make a point of drawing attention to it.

Before Riley could continue her conversation, Piper's mother rushed into Starbucks and began waving her arms trying to get Piper's attention.

"Piper," she whispered but it wasn't a real whisper, more like she was spraying out air with compressed spittle.

Piper cringed. She knew she had to leave for her soccer game, but she wanted to hear Riley.

"Mom, please!" begged Piper standing up and trying not to be noticed. "I will be right out. Go on to the car! Pu-leeze, Mom!" Piper's cheeks were red with embarrassment.

"Fine, honey," cooed Mrs. Deleve, "but you gotta hurry up because the clock is ticking, and we cannot be late. You know how the coach gets so daggone angry at you!"

Piper sat down in a huff and her mother quietly turned around and left.

Piper looked up at Riley, apologetically and said, "Please go on, Riley, before my mother makes another grand entrance!"

Riley knew her time was limited so she spoke rapidly. "Okay, here it is. We still do not know why exactly Mr. DeWitt was pulled out. I have my suspicions, but I am not going to share them right now.

"All I can tell you is that when Cindy and Jilly and I were talking with Dr. LIbertino, and she was genuinely cool about all of this, well, she said she wanted to know what we thought of Mr. DeWitt. Not just about his teaching, but about how he interacted with all of us?"

Lucas stood up. "Riley, girl. Get to the point. Are you asking if Mr. DeWitt did anything wrong with anyone?"

Lucas walked up to where Riley was standing, turned, and faced the group. "Look, I know I have been having my personal issues this year…"

"This year, Lucas?" Tommy jumped in. "You mean every year."

Lucas coughed. "Okay, asshole, yeah, I've had some problems. But today isn't about me; it's about Mr. DeWitt. And if you ask me, well, shit, I need to ask all of you." Lucas slowed down and looked at each one in their group one by one, slowly.

"Okay, I'm not going to sugarcoat this stuff. Did Mr. DeWitt touch any one of you the wrong way? Did he say something to you that was like ya know, he shouldn't have said that made you feel creepy? Cause these are all the reasons he would have been yanked out like that."

Jáquan stood up. "How come you know shit like this, Lucas? Did your father tell you?"

Lucas pressed his lips tightly together and clenched his hands into tight fists. "No," he said with venom in his voice. "First of all, he's not my goddamned father and secondly, c'mon, man, you read the papers, you see it in the news. It's pretty obvious, don't ya think?"

Riley knew she had to take control of the group, or it was going to dissolve as quickly as a snowball on a hot day. "Okay, enough. Let me get back to it, please? Lucas, thanks, but I got it from here. You can go back to your seat.

"Here's the deal. I need every one of you. And I mean every one of you to go home today and write an email to Dr. Libertino telling her exactly what you think of Mr. DeWitt as a teacher, a mentor, hell – a friend if you want to. But be especially careful because things have been said about him that are not good. I'm not going to go into those details because I am only going on the insinuations that Dr. LIbertino kind of, sort of hinted at. And it's going to be up to us to prove that he is a decent, caring teacher who has done NOTHING, and I repeat NOTHING inappropriate to any of us."

Cindy started crying loud enough that all eyes suddenly turned on her.

Mateo stood up. "What the f…, Cindy? Are you okay? What's going on with you?"

Cindy swiped at her nose, rubbed her eyes, and faced the group. "I think it's my fault."

Jilly grabbed Cindy's arm and yanked her down. It was Jilly's turn. She knew she had to say something, so she stood up.

"Look, we all joke around and what Cindy is trying to say is that she goofed around saying how weird Mr. DeWitt was, but she meant it in a good way. We think some teacher heard her and used that against Mr. DeWitt. Which is why we need all of you to write to Dr. L. today.

"It's not Cindy's fault. She didn't do anything wrong. I think someone didn't like him and used that against him. If we don't speak up, we may never see him again. Is that what we want? Can you live with that? Can you live without taking responsibility for someone's career and taking action?"

Sofia didn't realize that she popped out of her seat and yelled, "Yeah! Right on, Jilly! I'm gonna do it!"

Junay raised her hand. When Riley rolled her eyes at her, she put her hand down and said indignantly, "Are we going to get in trouble for doing this? You know I cannot get in trouble. It is not part of my DNA."

There were moans and groans from the group and Junay coughed and went back to reading her manual.

The manager of Starbucks, an older balding man in his 40s, was suddenly behind Riley. "Uhhh, excuse me group, but you're getting kinda loud over here. Are you all done with your drinks and food, or do you need to order something else? Otherwise, maybe it's time for you to head out and let some other people have a seat over here, huh?"

Lucas refused to be bullied. "Who do you think you are, huh, man? We can sit here all day and…"

Max stood up and said very quietly but with a newfound authority, "Uhh, so sorry, sir. We have all finished and we are just about to leave your establishment. Thank you for having us. You have a good day, but would you tell that barrister over there that next time he makes a macchiato Frappuccino he should use fewer ice cubes and more syrup, okay? Like it was really watery, man.

"Okay, I'm done, now. Thank you." And Max sat down, grinning from ear to ear.

It was Piper's turn. "Thanks, guys. I'm outta here, but Riley, I'm with you. I will be writing that email as soon as I get home from my game."

"Thanks, Piper. And hey, let's all get on our social media and spread the word – the more of us who can send an email to our principal, the better."

Whitney took a deep breath and shouted out, "Everyone – let's thank Riley for doing this for Mr. DeWitt. And Cindy and Jilly, too!"

The group clapping and stomping, got up in unison, grabbed their trash, and shuffled out of Starbucks, leaving the manager to close his eyes and shake his head. "Damn teenagers," he said to no one as he wiped down the tables that were left in disarray.

CHAPTER 21

Linette stepped out of the shower, her bleached white hair soaking wet and dripping all over the tiled bathroom floor. Linette automatically dropped her towel and used it to wipe the growing puddle on the floor grasping the faded blue cotton cloth with her toes and using it as the handle to her mopping.

Linette stared into the fogged mirror, casually wiping away the condensation caused by her super-hot shower. An image reflected back at her. She tilted her head examining the stranger looking back at her. Who was she?

Linette, the good daughter. Linette, the good girl. Linette, the good friend. Linette the good student, well most of the time when she studied which wasn't often because she was distracted. Too distracted to study, but too torn inside to unpack her true feelings that caused all the anxieties.

Linette had just finished writing to her principal, Dr. Libertino. She did as she was told. She liked the kids in her mentoring class even though she did not hang out with them outside the school day. She felt a connection with them in ways she never felt before so when she was asked to do this assignment, Linette knew she would have no trouble writing about Mr. DeWitt. She had written many glowing comments about her favorite teacher. He was kind to her even when she was especially quiet and downright sullen in their afternoon mentoring program.

She knew she needed the program. Too often Linette retreated into her private and secret world. It was a world her single mom would never understand. Even her few friends were puzzled by her because she didn't share the same interests. Her friends were all Filipino, but only because they were Filipino and that was where the commonality ended. She refused to go to their church; she refused to listen to their music or watch their movies. She argued with her mother about the foods she cooked begging her mom to be more American, more like everyone else.

More American. What was that anyway? Was it like the silly television shows she watched? Was it the perfect kids on the Nickelodeon series that she tried to imagine herself being on one day?

In her spare time, Linette poured over her anime comic books, often creating artwork into her sketchbook that was overflowing with her drawings, her designs, her life, and even her dreams.

Who was she kidding? She spoke Tagalog with her mother because her mother still struggled to learn English. Together they came to America only thirteen years ago because her uncle sponsored them. And so they moved here with the barest of belongings. They had left her biological father behind – whom she had met only once, and now no one knew where he lived – even if he was still alive. Linette barely remembered what he looked like except for an old cracked picture she found hidden in her mother's jewelry box. Her mother refused to talk about him and so Linette gave up asking about him.

And now what? Linette was the star that the family hung their gilded ropes on. She was the one who was going to make everyone proud. Go to school. Go to college. Become a doctor. Get married and have many little Filipino babies. Oh, wait, that meant marrying someone who was Filipino. Now how was that going to happen when she purposely separated herself from that circle?

Linette stared in the mirror again, her body finally dried from the air even though the towel on the floor was still soaking up small pools of water. Linette tried to be objective as she stared at the reflection.

Yeah. Who am I? A young girl about to be a woman? What if I don't want to be a woman? What if I don't want to be a man? What if I don't know who I want to be at all? Dear God, Dear Allah, Dear Bathalah, Dear Jesus Christ, oh, I don't know who to pray to.

Suddenly, Linette stared at her heap of shower stuff thrown haphazardly in a wooden box on the counter: soaps, creams, deodorant, and there it was: her razor. Without a moment's hesitation, Linette swooped her pink razor blade up, grabbed the right side of her hair, and started shaving. Clumps of hair floated noiselessly into the sink, their wet whiteness blending into oblivion within the white ceramic basin.

The more Linette shaved, the wider her grin grew. Satisfied with the shaven look on her one side, Linette threw the razor blade carelessly into her sink and picked up her purple shears. She grabbed the hair in the back of her head and started clipping, not caring where the hair fell or how much she was cutting.

It felt like hours flew by when in reality the cutting took only ten minutes and suddenly just as quickly as she had started Linette threw the scissors in the sink.

"There!" She whispered triumphantly. "Now, just like the butterfly emerges from its cocoon, so shall I emerge newly hatched, newly named, and newly discovered."

Linette grabbed handfuls of tissues, dampened them, and quickly wiped up all of her dropped hair, her old disintegrated persona. She cleaned the sink, the floor, and everywhere she found pieces of her hair. It was as if she were wiping herself clean and transpiring into a new person.

Finished, and quite satisfied, Linette dressed herself in a pair of her loosest jeans and an oversized shirt.

She took out her cell phone, breathed in slowly and cautiously, and clicked her camera icon to take a selfie.

Linette liked what she saw so she uploaded it to her Instagram page and labeled it for the first time:

Welcome, Lane, everyone. Please refer to me as they/them from today on till…whenever.

Lane sat down at her desk, opened her sketch pad to a new page, and drew a self-portrait. She took her time, using charcoal and different shades of special pencils. Her smile never left her face. She felt newly born.

"There I am. My name is Lane and today is the first day of the rest of my life. Amen!"

CHAPTER 22

Carl stared at his younger brother as if seeing him for the first time. They had been driving for over an hour in complete silence – a vast abyss that had grown and widened over time. Any hope of a bond had been cemented years ago. Carl noticed that Chip's brown hair was thinning and there were a few early-onset gray streaks. His sharp peacock blue eyes looked watery and dull behind the contacts.

The two of them were on a mission, going to see their possibly dying mother, but not as brothers, no, they were strangers to each other as time and hurt and lack of communication had forged a brick wall so high it was not scalable.

Carl turned his head staring straight ahead. Praying this day would end soon and that seeing his mother would ease some of his pain.

Now it was Chip who turned and stared at his brother. There were so many times Chip wanted to reach out to his brother, apologize to him for so many things, and pray that the two of them could become allies if not friends.

"Look, Carl," Chip faltered and started over. He gripped the steering wheel and pretended to focus on the traffic. "I know things haven't been always good between us…"

Carl interrupted almost whispering, "Always? How about never? You were such an egotistical selfish brat who wanted nothing to do with me. Ever. Forever the star athlete, the star of the family, the star of…" Carl breathed in sharply, almost choking. He didn't realize how long he wanted to say that to Chip. His head dropped on his chest and he closed his eyes. "I'm sorry, Chip," Carl quickly caught his breath and wiped his nose which had started running.

"Look, it wasn't your fault that dad put all his eggs in your basket. I get it. I was the family nerd, the loner, the loser. And poor Emma." Carl sucked in his breath as he wept easily just saying his sister's name. Carl sniffed hard, swallowed, and started again, "And poor goddamn Emma was just trying to find herself and she never could. She fucking never could because she had no one to support her. Not you, not mom, and not dad. I tried, but even I could not get through to her. To let her know that she was a good and decent human being. Damn it all, Chip. We failed her. I failed her and I will never forgive myself for that. She took her own life. She was alone and scared and hurting. She should never have felt that way.

"And every day I go to work, I make sure that I let my students know they are good and worthwhile no matter what they look like or sound like or even if they failed an exam or didn't make the team. I sure as hell never made the team and I know how that hurts. You never get over that. You never stop remembering the hurt, but you go on and over time…," Carl stopped to catch his breath. "Over time, you realize that none of that matters. What matters is to be the best human being you can be, to be kind to others, and make sure if someone is hurting that you listen to them and reassure them that they are going to be okay."

Chip squeezed his lips together. With one hand curled into a fist, he pummeled himself in the forehead, several times. Defeated. He knew he had to open up and share some things with Carl. He had to before it was too late.

"Carl," Chip looked quickly at Carl and then back again at the road. He spoke so softly that Carl leaned towards him. "Look, I cannot make up for all those years. I wish I could. I never wanted to be a star. I hated it. Dad was always forcing me to join every team I could. He would berate me in front of the coaches telling them to beat my ass if I didn't cooperate or didn't give it my best no matter how I felt.

"Why do you think I was never home? I stayed away as much as I could because the minute I was home dad was on my case asking me how my practice was or why didn't I score or why did I let the basketball guard stuff me? Over and over again. And if he didn't like my answer, he would call me a pussy who would never achieve anything in life. He said if I didn't make him proud because I was an athlete than I would always be a nobody, a nothing. And worse, he said if he couldn't brag about me to his friends, then he would have to brag about his other son who he called the genius of the family."

Carl jerked his head up so abruptly he heard his neck crack. "What are you talking about? He hated me. I was the loser, not you!"

Chip laughed. "See, that's what I mean. He played us against each other. You were the brains, and I was nothing but a jock he could boast about to his friends. Hell, Carl, I was so embarrassed when he would come to my games. He would yell and scream and sometimes shout obscenities if the call didn't go my way. One time I heard the referee say to Coach that if that crazy man in the bleachers didn't shut up, he was going to forfeit our game."

Carl's mouth opened and shut. He didn't know what to say. Finally, he blurted out, "And where did that leave Emma?"

"Oh," said Chip, "that's really easy. Dad blamed everything about Emma on mom. Emma was just like mom, according to dad, a slut who would eventually have to have a shot gun wedding like theirs. And every night that Emma was not around, dad would curse at mom as though it was all her fault and swear she was out making babies just like mom did to snare some poor jerk into marrying her.

"Poor Emma never had a chance. Carl, I know you tried. Emma wrote to me, too, you know. She told me how you were always there for her, trying to get her to stay home, to finish school, to make something out of herself so she could leave and have her own beautiful life. But she was determined to run away and find some scraps of happiness out there. I guess….," Chip sobbed, grabbed his water bottle and slugged it down quickly, coughing a bit. He continued, "I guess she never found that happiness. I'm just so sorry that you were the one who had to deal with it at the end."

Carl didn't stop the tears that were sluicing down his cheek, slipping through his days-old facial stubble and falling off his face.

"Chip, I didn't know you were there for her, too. It's too bad we couldn't have worked together and brought her home. I wanted to so badly. So badly, but I failed."

"No, Carl," Chip said softly, consoling his brother, "No, it wasn't because of you or me. Emma was a lost soul and try as she might, she could not find herself. We didn't know better. We didn't know how to save her. That's why, that's why…."

Carl looked at Chip. "What are you talking about, Chip? Huh?"

Chip breathed deeply, his chest rising and falling as though he were trying to gain some inner strength.

"Carl," Chip faltered and started again, his hands clenching the wheel for courage, "Carl, after you graduated college and started working and moved out, I was aimless. I couldn't find myself. I know exactly how Emma felt.

"So, I tried junior college for a while, playing on their football team only because they gave me some scholarship money. Hearing dad screaming in the stadium every week only made me angry. I couldn't take it anymore. I quit."

Carl picked up his water and swallowed large amounts of water so he wouldn't have to answer right away. He wanted to hear everything, and he did not want Chip to think he was judging him.

Chip continued. "I got involved with a girl. I thought she was super hot and I wanted out of sports, out of college, and out on my own. Her name is Tarynda and I thought she was the sun and the moon and my whole new world. So Tary and I moved into a very cheap run-down apartment and I started working at Dick's Sporting Goods Store. I figured I knew everything about sports, ya know?

"Well, next thing I know Tary is pregnant, so we rush off to the justice of the peace, get married, and then we break it to mom and dad and her parents. No one, I mean no one is happy with either of us, so we felt so alone. Anyway, Tary has a little girl."

Carl hiccuped, burped, and smiled all at once. "Yay! My little brother. Hey, I'm an uncle. Whoooo hooooo, Chip that's so awesome. When can I see her, and hey, what's her name?

Chip wiped his nose with the back of his hand. "She's going to be two years old next month. She's with her babysitter right now because Tary, well, Tary did not want to be a mom right now. She filed for divorce a month after she gave birth and left me and gave me full custody of our girl. She packed up and moved to…to…hell, I don't even know.

"And, Carl?"

"Yeah, Chip?"

"I named her Emma."

CHAPTER 23

Barbara had just finished showing Mr. Netsworth where the new school cameras were going to be installed. Satisfied with her directions, Barbara headed back to her office. She was walking swiftly down the hall and around the corner hoping to get back so she could complete her work when she was suddenly body-slammed by Alisa Saper, the foods teacher. Alisa's gentle brown eyes were teary, and her hands were shaking and she could not stop apologizing to Barbara as she followed her into the office.

"Please sit down, Ms. Saper. What can I do for you? You seem upset. Did something happen? Was it a student? A parent? Please, please have a seat, and let's talk." Barbara guided Alisa over to her round table and helped her to her seat.

Barbara turned and walked over to her door, leaned out, and looked for Joanne, her secretary. Joanne, who was only working that day to help Barbara, must have felt those *Ineedyou* vibrations as she suddenly appeared in the hall. Barbara put her fingers to her lips and then touched her eyes signifying tears. Joanne immediately recognized the do-not-disturb taciturn message, nodded her head, and returned to her desk.

Closing the door gently, Barbara scooped up her box of tissues and placed them next to Alisa as she sat down next to her. This was not a conversation that needed to be held from across her desk, and Barbara knew when familiarity was more important than authority.

Alisa let her shoulders sag and new tears flowed softly down her cheeks. Her braids, let loose since she was not in the teacher/cooking mode, surrounded her heart-shaped face as though it were a protective shield.

"I…I…" Alisa started and stopped. But she knew she had to continue. She felt an obligation from, well, she wasn't sure where that origin was, but she was compelled to speak. And so she started anew.

"Ms. Atkinson. I…uh…I am not sure where to begin, so I'm going to ramble for a bit if you don't mind."

Barbara did not want to interrupt her, so she nodded lightly. She wanted to reach out and hold Alisa's hand for support but held back. Not yet, she thought.

"I know there are many teachers who do not like Mrs. Winewrought. I mean, for whatever reasons they may have. I hear the gossip. I hear the comments from kids and even some of the parents. I know that Beverly, Mrs. Winewrought, and I have been close over the past few years. You know, we talk, we text, we go out to Starbucks and even dinner sometimes. So I see a whole different side of her. I see the gentle, caring side of her.

"And lately, uh, to tell you the truth, it's been since school began. I guess it's when you announced that Mr. DeWitt and Mrs. Waverly were the teachers in charge of the mentoring program. That is when I saw Beverly change. Seriously change. Like claws came out of her that I never saw before. She was angry all the time. All. The. Time."

Barbara felt the need to talk before this confession took a different turn. Was Alisa going to share something so private that would put the both of them in a compromising position? Would Barbara have to tell someone? What would be those repercussions?

"Ms. Saper?"

"It's okay. I know that whatever I tell you now you might have to go forward with this. And I've been struggling with this for weeks. And I can't hold it in any longer. It's tearing me up inside. I can't sleep. I can't eat. Damn, I'm having problems in the classroom because I'm having trouble focusing."

Barbara reached over to take Alisa's hand. "It's okay, Alisa. I'm here for you. Whatever you tell me we will work together on the situation. I cannot sit here and allow you to go through this alone any longer. Please, go ahead. Tell me." Barbara got up, walked over to her small refrigerator in the corner of her office, opened it, and took out two water bottles. She came back to her table, handed Alisa one, and then opened hers and started drinking.

Alisa nodded, opened her bottle, and took a long, slow drink. She began gradually.

"It started with a few snide remarks about Carl. Mr. DeWitt. How he was so involved with his kids. How he knew so much about them, where they liked to go on the weekends, what sports they were involved in, what music groups, their hobbies. She kept whining that knowing that stuff was not natural, not right. I disagreed with her because he was just that kind of a guy who was genuinely interested in his students. But she would not listen to me.

"And then she kept repeating what other students were saying about Mr. DeWitt. How he was 'weird' and that seemed to be the green light for her. She grabbed onto that word and well, honestly, it spiraled out of control. She even spied on the mentoring class after school until Scott Sheldrake questioned her."

Barbara leaned forward. "How do you know that Mr. Sheldrake questioned her?"

Alisa sighed. "Because I was in my room after school working with my cooking club kids. Mr. Sheldrake happened to walk in and asked if he could use my sink. I said of course and looked at him. He shrugged and whispered to me that Mrs. Winewrought had just spit on him in the hallway."

"No!" Barbara whistled incredulously. "I wonder why he never told me about that incident."

"He told me because he knew Beverly and I were close and perhaps I could tell him why she was so angry. I played dumb and said I didn't know."

Barbara downed the rest of her water bottle and put it down softly on the table. "That's okay. Don't feel bad. I can understand why you did not want to get into all that teacher gossip. What else?"

Alisa closed her eyes. Her lips started quivering and she forced herself to continue. "There is so much more. So much more."

And for the next hour, Alisa let it all out. She showed Barbara all of her text messages. She confessed about knowing that Beverly's husband had hurt her and left bruises, but that Beverly always hid them under her lab coat. She told Barbara that Beverly moved in with her for a short time. Beverly finally left when she decided it was necessary to confront Ted about everything.

"Ms. Atkinson? Beverly lied. She lied about Carl. She lied about him being inappropriate. She lied about everything, and I feel like it's my fault for not coming to you sooner." Alisa started choking and sobbing at the same time and could not stop. It was as if a giant weight had been lifted from her shoulders and the release was so traumatic that she started convulsing and could not stop.

Barbara took her arm and slid it around Alisa's shoulders and squeezed as though this motion would erase all of her bad feelings.

"Shhhh, Alisa. It's okay. You told me all you need to tell me. I am going to take it from here. Now let me walk you to your car. Go home. Relax. It's going to be alright. I am going to make sure it will be alright. You have my word. I promise you. Thank you, Alisa. Thank you for coming forward. This took a lot of courage and I cannot tell you how special you are for taking this on. You are very brave."

Alisa sniffed, wiped her nose with a tissue, and then dabbed at her tear-stained dark brown eyes. "I am so sorry it has come to this. I am so sorry. I am…."

Barbara stood up. "No, don't worry. Now, come along. Let me walk with you. Are you okay driving home? Do you want me to follow you?"

Alisa shook her head. "No, I'll be okay. And Ms. Atkinson, thank you. Thank you for listening to me."

Barbara helped Alisa out of her chair and slid her arm through hers. "C'mon, let's walk into the fresh air. You did the right thing, Alisa. And I know this was hard, but it's over now. This is going to be all cleared up very soon."

Together they left her office and walked out, passing Joanne. Joanne looked up quizzically at Barbara, but Barbara only nodded at her. Joanne smiled and went back to work.

When Barbara returned to the office, she stopped at Joanne's desk and said, "Call Mr. Sheldrake down here. I need to talk to him immediately. And, Joanne, after that go on home. Thank you for coming in today. You have been a huge help to me. But now I need you to start your vacation and get some rest because when you come back you and I are going to be very, very busy!!"

CHAPTER 24

It was very early in the morning and there was a cold chill in the December winter air. Cindy blew on her hands to warm them as she stood in front of the large door. Large puffs that looked like small balls of clouds emerged from Cindy's mouth. She wanted to knock on the door. She seriously needed to, but her anxiety was so high she could barely breathe. And so she stood there, frozen like the trees and plants surrounding her. If the wind gusted hard enough, she would crack in two.

Suddenly the door flew open and a very attractive woman with deep dove gray eyes and short brown hair with a few silver streaks stood in front of her. She was the spitting image of Riley except for the color of her eyes, and it made Cindy step back almost falling off the front porch step.

"Well, hello, young lady," laughed Jeanine Maddox. You must be Cindy. Riley said she was having a friend over today. I didn't mean to yank the door open on you so abruptly! I was running out to warm up the car this morning and goodness gracious – there you were."

Riley, hearing the commotion at her front door, came running over. "Mom, this is Cindy, but I guess you figured that out. Cindy, come in out of the cold, girl. And take off your puffy coat; jeez it's not that cold outside!"

Cindy smiled, but her cheeks were so cold she felt as if she gave one of the fake movie star smiles. She stared up into the warm face of Riley's mom. "Uh, hello, Dr. Maddox."

Jeanine turned around and said to Riley, "Oh, honey, is this the girl you want me to talk about who is having such bad cramps? Huh?"

"Momm-a!" screeched Riley. "Really? Do you have to go there? Right now? Right here? Puleeze! And NO, this is not who I was talking to you about. Listen, Cindy is going to be here for a few days, okay? I'll explain later. You and Dad go on to work and I will make sure dinner is ready for the both of you. If you are going to be late, text me and I'll keep your dinner warm, okay?"

Jeanine smiled at her only daughter, leaned over, and hugged her so tightly Riley coughed out a mmmpphhh. "Mom, you and Dad really need to go. Cindy and I have a project we are working on. Okay?"

Jeanine unleashed her tight grip on her daughter slowly as if releasing her was like giving her child permission to grow up. Riley was maturing too quickly for Jeanine, but she had no control over that. It was inevitable. Sometimes

Jeanine would stare at Riley and force herself to remember her as a little toddler chewing on her fingers or as a young girl on the soccer field flying down the field to score yet again. It was all happening too suddenly for Jeanine, and she felt her eyes tear up. The cold air stifled the flow that was threatening to spill over. Jeanine sniffed in the frigid air.

"Okay, my baby girl. Get back in the house. Tell Daddy I'm ready for him. You and Cindy have a great day together. We'll talk later, okay? And remember to bring down the decorations from the attic. I want to decorate the house with you. Just like we always do. I love you, sweet girl. Okay, gotta run."

And with that, Dr. Jeanine Maddox switched gears into doctor mode so visibly you could actually see the physical mechanics of her body language working.

Riley's dad, Dr. Gunther Maddox came charging down the stairs in a hurry. His blonde, thinning hair was still wet from his early shower and his clothes hung on him like he had been on a rapid weight loss program. He smiled at Riley, his tight lips blowing her a kiss as his deep amber eyes twinkled at his beloved daughter.

"Love you, pumpkin, I do," he chimed at her. "And your nice friend, too. We'll see you later, Dragonbreath. Be a good girl and don't eat too much junk today." He winked at her before he exited the door. "But if you've got a hankering for some special dark chocolate with raspberry jelly I hid it in my office behind the Good Health book. Hah hah, and cheerio, my love."

And another Maddox left the building. Riley shut the door for her father, turned around, and leaned into the door for more strength. She looked at Cindy.

"And that was a long conversation today! So you see, Cindy, it's not always so peachy keen across town now is it?"

Cindy's crystal blue eyes were wide open behind her thick black glasses. She pushed her bangs up against her forehead and whistled. "Whew! That was exhausting, wasn't it?"

"Yeah, well, I'm used to it, I guess. So what do you want to do first? How about we make some breakfast? I am in the mood for chocolate chip pancakes with some bacon on the side. How about you?"

"Oh, wow. I usually eat cold cereal and a burnt piece of toast if I'm lucky in the morning. My mom is out the door early to get to the grocery store for work. She is always the first one there to work the register. Sometimes they let her fill out paperwork in the office and she gets pretty excited about learning some new stuff.

"So, yeah, pancakes and bacon are totally cool. If it's cool with you that is."

"Okay, go put your things in the bedroom upstairs on the right. That's the guest room and you'll be comfortable there. How long do you want to stay?"

"Well, my mom is going to have her first chemo treatment starting tomorrow and she doesn't want me to watch over her. She says she may have to throw up a lot and she's afraid I'll just panic. That's gross, isn't it? Thanks, Riley, for letting me stay with you. This holiday break is not what I thought would be."

"Hell, it never is for me so this is fine." Riley turned and headed into the kitchen to start breakfast.

Cindy grabbed her book bag and her duffle bag. She couldn't help staring at all the paintings on the wall, the furnished rooms filled with overstuffed chairs and large comfy-looking couches. Cindy was overwhelmed with the opulence of Riley's home as she plodded up the stairs weighed down with her belongings.

Cindy walked into the guest room, dropped her belongings on the bed, and plopped down on a huge bean bag chair. Tears sprung out of her eyes. She didn't want to be here. She wanted to be with her mother, helping her, holding her, hugging her. But her mother insisted she stay with somebody, anybody. Cindy couldn't think of anyone who would even allow her to stay, especially during the holiday. She practically begged Riley on the last day of school. Riley finally gave in telling her that if she bugged her one time she was going to kick her out.

Cindy had nowhere to go. She and her mom could never afford to live in a house furnished like this. She was lucky they had their small townhome with hand-me-down furniture they bought at the used furniture store on the other side of town. Cindy let the tears flow freely. She saw the box of tissues on the dresser and immediately grabbed a few. She blew her nose, wiped her eyes, and stood up.

"Okay, Cindy. It's time to grow up. Mom has cancer.

She's handling it. But I need to handle it, too. I'll be tough for you, Mom. I promised you, didn't I?" And with a new determination, Cindy left the bedroom and went downstairs to see how she could help Riley.

CHAPTER 25

Beverly was driving without thinking. She knew where she was going. It was an internalized muscle memory. A memory she hated with all her heart. The highway roads shifted gradually into back roads and the newly developed mega mansions stood naked and lost in their new lawns bereft of the trees that used to tickle the clouds above and fill the air with their large oxygen-producing leaves and homes that used to be occupied by many birds, insects, and squirrels. But now their natural habitat was ripped out of the earth to take the place of the new inhabitants who wanted little to do with their environment other than to say that they wanted to protect it which, if you think about it those giant trees have now been transformed into planks of wood or paper or mulch somewhere else in the world.

Darlene Stevenson, small, short gray-haired, and mousy looking with dull gray eyes and a slight hunchback stood restlessly at her screen door. She was anxiously awaiting her daughter's return. She had not seen Beverly in months – ever since her husband, Jack, had passed away from a massive heart attack while mowing the lawn in early July.

"Jack! Don't mow today," she had cried to him that morning. Jack was already looking pale, his beady dark eyes bloodshot from drinking too much bourbon the night before.

"Aww, leave me alone, woman," Jack snapped back at her. He was always snapping, never listening to anyone. His tall frame was dwarfed by his larger-than-life ego, and he refused advice, help, or suggestions from anyone who would still even try to converse with him. He was a stubborn, ignorant bully. He hated his neighbors, his sister, his former boss, and at times his wife. He tolerated his wife only because he intimidated her into being submissive. His daughter Beverly was another story. She was built like him, stubborn, a fighter. He liked that but he hated her husband. Ted was a weeny, at least that's what Jack called him behind his back. He ignored Ted as much as he ignored everyone else and that suited him just fine.

But on that fatal day in July Jack refused to listen to anyone telling him that the temperature was off the roof. It was going to be in the 100s with an incredibly high humidity and a chance of severe thunderstorms later in the afternoon. But Jack would not listen.

"I'm going to mow my goddamn lawn before it rains and ain't nobody gonna tell me different." He had preached to Darlene enough times when he was determined to do something, and she was finally tired of arguing.

"Go on," she said with no love in her voice. "Go on and I'll be damned if I'm the one who will be calling 911 when you drop like a rock on that danged old mower that you won't trade in for a ride-on. You're an old man with a bad ticker. But, hell, go on since you won't listen to me." And then under her breath, she muttered to no one but herself, "And I'll be the first one to tell I told you so, you old bastard when you drop dead on me! And just you wait to see what I'm planning on doing with your insurance money – you old fart!"

Jack was dead in the middle of the yard at high noon having collapsed from severe dehydration and a massive heart attack that hit him so hard and so fast he never had time to cry out, "Oh, God, save me!"

Beverly slowed her car down, turned into the driveway, and spotted her mother pacing in front of the screen door. She knew her mother was lonely since Beverly's father passed away, but she hated coming home. Hated the memories that always came flooding back poisoning any shreds of happy childhood recollections.

"C'mere, Jellybean!" her father shouted at her. It was his nickname for her since she was always stuffing jellybeans in her mouth from the time she could chew.

It was right after her tenth birthday. Beverly had been given a brand-new sleeping bag and she was so proud of it she couldn't wait to show it off with her friends at the sleepover. Beverly slowly shuffled into the living room cautious of what was about to happen. It always seemed to happen to her. It was inevitable. She was clumsy; she was awkward. That's what occurs when you are always the tallest in the class. Her mother tried to console her but to no avail. Beverly slid into the small chair in the corner hiding from big Jack's malevolent stare.

"Okay, now, girlie. Where is my glass jar filled with all those marbles I collected from the yard sale last week? Huh? It was right on this table next to my chair. MY chair that you are not allowed to sit in? Huh? I'm asking you! Where is the jar?"

Beverly was squirming. "I....I....didn't mean to do it, Daddy. Honest! I was walking by and it was my new sleeping bag that I was carrying from my sleepover and it was too big and I...I....oh, Daddy, I guess I knocked over the jar and it kinda broke and..."

"Kinda broke? Kinda broke? Where the hell are all those marbles I bought? I had a special collection and now where is it?"

But before Beverly could open her mouth to explain to her enraged father that her mother had helped her pick up every single shard of broken glass. Then the two of them had carefully found every runaway marble and had hidden them in a bag until Beverly could replace the jar. And suddenly, Jack was looming larger than life in front of her.

Whack! The smack across her face came so quickly and stung so intensely that Beverly saw stars. Her head was woozy, and she felt as though she was about to black out. She fell back against the chair, her hand gently touching the burning flesh of her cheek.

"Don't you ever lie to me again or I will make sure you will be outside picking up every weed in the entire lawn with a damned paper grocery bag!"

Beverly, sniffing back tears that were racing down her swollen face, cried out, "I didn't lie, Daddy. I just didn't get a chance to…"

Jack lifted his large hand poised to come swinging down even harder when Darlene came running into the room.

"Get your hand away from her this instant!" she screamed. Beverly, sweetie, go on up to your room. I'll deal with your father. Go! Now!"

Beverly did not have to be told twice. She raced past her father and up to her room where she closed the door, locked it, and flopped on her bed letting the pain and the tears swim together.

Beverly, still sitting in her car, shook her head trying to sweep away that memory. She turned off the car, got out, and walked slowly to her mother. While Darlene had a huge smile on her face, Beverly knew it was all for show. It was always for show.

CHAPTER 26

Lila sat in her home office pondering. What was to be done? The holiday week was almost over, and she could not stop reading the emails from her students. Emails that kept pouring in that were filled with honest heart-wrenching anecdotes proclaiming how Carl DeWitt was their favorite teacher. It was more than just a bunch of phony sentiments; it was genuine and touching. She could not stop reading them:

Hey, Dr. L.,

This is Max Hobler. I'm gonna tell you that Mr. DeWitt is the main reason I come to school every day. He makes sure I'm okay and always asks me about my dog cause he's old and has a heart problem. Don't take Mr. D. away. I need him

Good morning, Dr. Libertino,

Riley told me to write to you so here it is. Mr. DeWitt is my favorite teacher. He never makes me feel bad in class cause some of your other teachers call me stupid sometimes especially Mrs. Wine, I forget how to spell her name and she is not nice to me but Mr. DeWitt he always makes me believe in myself. Please don't get rid of him. I really like him and he has never said anything that's bad.

Your student, Tommy T

Lila couldn't help but laugh when she read:

Hello, Principal Libertino,

It is with great urgency that I write to you due to circumstances beyond our control causing with great disappointment that you have removed a most benevolent and positive teacher named Mr. DeWitt. He has the utmost respect for every student, and even though I am one of the top students in the 9th grade he never makes fun of me even if I question him on a fact or two. You see I plan on being president of the class and I have to know my history and he understands my focus and determination. Oh, back to Mr. DeWitt, he is always a perfect gentleman towards everyone.

Who said he wasn't? I would like to know who started that rumor. We as teenagers cannot be overcome by such falsehoods. Really? Thank you for your time. See you when we return to school and I hope and pray Mr. DeWitt is back with us.

Your future president of the class, Junay Phame

Lila had to wipe away tears from laughing so hard at Junay's email. She certainly is focused, thought Lila. But it was the email from Lucas that tore at her heartstrings.

Hey,

I know I haven't been the best student this year and maybe I am learning to control my anger and all and I am even going to see that lady thera something you told me I had to see. I'll see her and all. But I'm writing to you because we heard that you fired Mr. DeWitt and I think you are wrong for doing that. Mr. DeWitt is a good guy. He doesn't curse in class he doesn't make you feel like you can't learn the shi I mean the stuff we need to know and he makes really dumb jokes that we laugh at because they are so dumb. He talks to me like I am somebody and not just another kid in his class he has to teach. We talk sports and we talk music and we talk about how he knows what it's like to feel alone in a school and we talk about me having some problems with my stepdad but he never tells me what to do he just listens to me no matter what I have to say and he never makes me feel bad when I tell him I don't like my stepdad and I wish I could live with my dad but not really and honest Dr. L. I have never seen Mr. DeWitt do anything that's wrong to anyone especially girls cause that always seems to be the problem now in schools I guess at least that's what my stepdad says. Please please don't fire him. He is the first teacher I have ever had in my whole life who saw me as Lucas and not Lucas the problem kid. We need him in our school. Please bring him back. Not just for me. For everyone.

Your student. Lucas.

Good afternoon, Dr. Principal,

My name is Mateo Ortiz but you can call me Mateo. I like Mr. Dewitt. He is a good man. He is a good teacher. I like him. I think I said that already. He makes me feel special in his class and not stupid when I dont know the answers. He says it is okay cause I am still lerning. Please do not get rid of him.

Mateo Ortiz

To my principal,

This is your student Whitney Shields and I am writing this email to inform you that someone has done a dirty to Mr. DeWitt. He is a good teacher and we all want him back. I know a good lawyer. He is my uncle. If I have to I can bring my uncle to school to see you in case this has to go to court. He tells me all the time all we have to do is to sue so I am ready if you feel that is the next best step.

I will be studying to be a lawyer when I grow up so this is a good practice for me.

Whitney

So many emails. So many stories. Who had started these accusations? Were there any students saying Carl was inappropriate? Lila had to think. She could not come up with any one instance anywhere and that truly disturbed her. Was it just one teacher who started all of this? And where was Carl's representative, Lemont Jacobs? How far has the investigation gone at this point? Time was going by too quickly.

And her son, Ben. His story about a teacher wrongfully accused. Her son had spoken up. She was immensely proud of her son for stepping up. And so, what about all of these students who have been emailing her nonstop? She was proud of them as well, but now what? Her head started throbbing. This was not the relaxing week she had been hoping for but then again, how was Carl faring in all of this? She needed to reach out to him and let her know how she felt about the situation and where it stands at this point in time. Was she allowed? What would happen if she did contact him? Too many questions and she was not sure she wanted to know the answers. Better to ask forgiveness later on than for permission, she always thought. Damn it all to hell!

CHAPTER 27

Lucas stared at the large brick building. It appeared foreboding and ugly and scary all at the same time. And he wanted no part of this. He wanted to be back in his own bed with the covers pulled over his head. He wanted to be anywhere but here. His long fingers gripped the door handle so tightly that his fingers went numb.

Julie, Lucas's mother, looked at him with sorrow in her eyes. There was a lump in her throat so large she was afraid to swallow. She knew this was hard for Lucas. No child should have to experience what Lucas had experienced with his father. It wasn't fair. What God in heaven allows fathers to hurt their children? Julie was torn and wanted to yank her gear shift from park to reverse and get the hell out of the parking lot. But she did not. She knew better. Lucas needed to deal with this, his demons. Demons? They were real, as real as it gets.

"Lucas?" Julie whispered. "Baby, it's time to go in. I'm going to go over to Starbucks for the next hour and then

I'll be back here waiting for you. Go on, my love. Take the first step and go."

Lucas turned and looked at this mother, his sapphire eyes as cold as the gemstone itself. "This is all your fault, Mom. If you hadn't married the asshole, he never would have…" Lucas could not finish his thoughts. It was too painful, too spiteful, and cruel and Lucas loved his mother too much to hurt her more than he already had done.

"Mom, I'm sorry…I…"

"Just go," Julie sobbed, her throat tight and hoarse from crying the night before. "Please, I beg you, just go up and see Miss Anna. You can tell her anything you want. I don't care. Blame me all you want, Lucas. It's okay. I deserve it. I should have known. I should have…"

Tears were streaming down Lucas's reddened cheeks, and he did not want his mother to see him crying. He jumped out of the car, slammed the door shut, and jogged to the door hoping she would leave. Quickly because in another minute he was going to turn around and run home.

Julie knew her son too well. She squeezed her eyes shut for just a moment, took a deep breath, swallowed very slowly, jerked the gear into reverse, and pulled out of her parking space. She wrenched the handle into drive and careened out of the parking lot.

Lucas turned around to see his mother racing out of the lot. He yanked the door open and went inside. *Grow up* he said to himself. *It's time you dealt with this. You can't keep running away and hiding in little playgrounds anymore.*

Courage is easy to feel when you are huddled together with a bunch of football players and you're screaming the next play. Courage is easy to believe when your coach grabs you by the shoulder pads and screams in your face that you're the best quarterback he has ever had in his career and now go throw a touchdown pass.

But courage is the first gut feeling to fly out of your soul when you have to pull open the door to those deep-seated dark memories. And Lucas hated going there. He shoved those incidents so entrenched inside him that a concrete drill would struggle to unleash them.

Lucas let his mind glaze over. He trudged up the stairs to the floor where his therapist was located. Cindy, who seemed to know he was going to see the same therapist, was all over him about how she loved Miss Anna and she loved her office and she loved the posters, and she….Jesus, that girl could talk the paint off the wall when she wasn't cringing in the corner of the cafeteria. Cindy made it a point to tell him she loved taking the stairs because it made her feel powerful and confident and holy hell, he couldn't get her to stop talking that day in Starbucks when the whole group of them met. And then she had to tell him all about the fact that Miss Anna was getting married over break and she was just coming back near the end of the break because she wanted to see everyone before school started and …"

"Uhhh, thanks, Cindy," Lucas finally interrupted. "I think I got it. Look, I'm not really into seeing this person, this, uhhh, whatever her name is, but I gotta go. Or else."

"Her name is Miss Anna and I absolutely love her! And what do you mean 'or else'? Or else what?"

Lucas did not want to go into the entire reason that his principal had told his mom why he was required to see the therapist. No one needed to know the real reason. Wasn't there a law for this or something like that?

"Hey, look, Cindy, I'll tell you what. When I go see this Anna lady, I will let you know how I like it, okay? And we're done talking, okay?"

Cindy shrugged. She wasn't comfortable talking to boys anyway and she thought that maybe she and Lucas would have something in common which would have made it easier to talk to him. But, guys, just forget them.

Lucas ignored her after that and now that he was trudging up the stairs that entire conversation with Cindy came cannonballing into his brain. I am so done with girls he thought. They drive me crazy.

Lucas located the office and slowly turned the handle and walked into the waiting room. He breathed a sigh of relief when he saw that no one was sitting there. He did not want to have a conversation with anyone, let alone in some headshrink's office.

He sat down and stared at the room. Okay, there's the poster Cindy likes and there is the poster she wants to buy for her bedroom. My Lord, that girl was too much on his brain.

The inner door opened and out strolled a young woman with long dark brown hair that was pulled back into a ponytail. She wore stylish glasses that were hanging on the edge of her long nose. Her big loop earrings glittered from the fluorescent lights in the ceiling.

Anna stuck her hand out to shake as she warmly greeted Lucas, "Hello. You must be Lucas, right?"

Lucas stood up a little too abruptly and almost knocked the chair over. He stuttered just a bit as he reached out to shake Anna's hand and said, "Uhhh, yeah…I'm….I'm Lucas. Lucas Cannon and …."

Anna interrupted him, "Hey, Lucas, why don't you go into my office where we can relax and get to know each other? Okay?"

Lucas stuck his hands in his pocket, looked down at the floor, and followed behind her. As soon as they entered her office, Anna pointed to a large comfortable chair and said, "Why don't you sit there, Lucas? It's big and comfy."

Lucas slumped into the chair and then puffed out his chest.

"Look, I know I gotta be here. I don't wanna be here. I don't wanna talk to you about anything and I got nothing to say. We can just sit here for as long as it takes for my mother to come pick me up and then I'm like peace out. Deal?"

Anna's hazel eyes squinted behind her glasses as she rubbed her chin slowly looking at Lucas as if sizing him up.

"Okay, then. First of all, my name is Anna Gorefield and you can call me Miss Anna. Yes, I recently got married over the holiday week if you're wondering why my name is different from the card you have crumbled up in your fist, but, oh, I can see you don't especially care about that.

So, Lucas Cannon, since you are here for the hour, let's get started. I am going to talk even if I'm the only one talking. But I have a feeling you're not going to want to just listen to me talk. So let me begin with…"

CHAPTER 28

Neva did not always enjoy school breaks. They were not the happiest of her memories. It was her first year of teaching. She had married Pooch – who has a nickname like that – right out of college. No fanfare, no crowd, just she and Ronnie ran off to the justice of the peace and said their vows. No honeymoon because there was no time. They would wait till they had money and a real job. Both English majors, or rather to be more specific Ronnie was a drama major. He was going to be an actor, a real actor on Broadway, and Neva would teach and support him until he made it big.

"Ronnie," she cooed. Oh, please, don't ever let me coo again she thought to herself. "Ronnie, honey," she begged. "C'mon to bed, baby. You've been rehearsing that same scene for hours, and if you don't know it by now you never will.

"I have an interview tomorrow morning and I need to nail it down so I can start teaching in the fall. So, come to bed, please!"

Ronnie bellowed, "I need to get it right! I am up against some real ringers for this part, and I don't want to blow it. Leave me be. I need to get into character."

And get into character he did. Every night. They grew further and further apart as he lost role after role and Neva was too busy writing lesson plans to worry about his shattered ego. He would grow a beard and when that didn't help he would shave it off. He would wear different colored contact lenses and when that didn't work any better, he gave them up. He would wear fake glasses and when that did not bring him any roles, he would throw them away. His bright aqua-blue eyes just got duller and less vibrant as the roles were rejected time and again.

And when Neva learned she was pregnant, Ronnie just shrugged and said, "I can play the part of a father. It's no big deal. But you'll have to keep working because I am very close to making it in this business."

Neva's pregnancy was short-lived. She miscarried early in the third month and Ronnie took that as an excuse to leave. "This is all too much for me to manage," he pleaded. "I need to focus on my career and being married and a father just doesn't leave me any room to grow my acting skills." He never thought about how Neva felt about losing the baby. Never comforted her those nights she cried herself to sleep. Never went with her to the doctor to see why she miscarried or to see if she could get pregnant again.

Ronnie moved out and Neva only learned he took an apartment in Hollywood when the divorce papers came to her from his California address. Neva signed the papers, kept her married name for no real reason except to prove that she once was married, mailed the divorce papers back, and never heard from Ronnie again. On a few occasions, she saw him peddling some vitamins in an infomercial late at night, but she never felt a tug at her heart, only regret for never carrying their baby to full term.

For some reason, during school breaks, Neva seemed to think back on the time when she was married and was almost a mom. It would have been very special, and the bittersweet memories only lasted till her break was over and then she tucked them way back into the recesses of her mind where romanticism and hopes and dreams once flourished.

Rather than think about Ronnie/Pooch man, Neva's mind was on Carl. He was someone special to her in a mentoring sort of way and she could not stand not knowing his status.

"Damn the rules once and for all," Neva said to Atticus, who only tilted his head in that I-think-I-know-what-you-are-saying and can I-have-a-treat-with-that?

Neva reached for her cell phone and without overthinking the repercussions, clicked on Carl's contact and hoped he would answer.

R.E.M.'s *Losing My Religion* came out loud and clear. "Damn him and his weird choice of songs!" cried Neva out loud. "Okay, Carl, my boy, here goes another one of my messages." Neva took a deep breath and began her message:

"Carl, hi, this is Neva. Remember me? Hahaha. So, I know I am not supposed to contact you, but I can't stand it any longer and you never answered my last text. I am very worried about you. I miss you. Are you alright? Do you need anything? We don't go back to school for another few days and if you feel like talking, please don't hesitate to call me or come on over. Atticus still misses you, too. Okay, I feel really awkward leaving messages, but I want you to know I care about you and, well, alright. I guess that's enough blabbering for now. Let me know you're ok even if it's just a text message. Take care, my friend. Bye."

• • •

At the same time, across town, Lila Libertino sat in her home office with her head in her hands. *Something does not add up,* she mused. Lila reached for another email.

Buenas noches. My name is Sofia and you don know me cause Im very quite girl in school. Im still learning to speak English but im the only one at home who can speak it. I want to tell it to you that Mr. Dawit is my favorite teacher. He don make fun of the way I talk and he don make fun of the way I write and he always ask me about my mama and papa and he always is polite. I can tell him many things and he never lafs at me and he never makes me feel bad about myself. I don know why he is not in school but the kids in my group tell me he did something bad. What he do? I never see him nothing. Please bring him back. I miss him and I need him bad.

Muchas gracias Sofia Ramos

Lila read and read till her eyes hurt from so many tears. By the time she was finished she knew what she had to do. She turned off her computer and reached for her cell phone.

"Hello, Lemont? This is Dr. Lila Libertino. Yes, I am fine, thank you for asking. I hope you are enjoying some downtime as well. Lemont? We need to talk because I think there has been a great injustice done to my teacher, Carl DeWitt. And it's high time we took care of it because I cannot allow this to continue."

CHAPTER 29

Beverly hugged her mother as tightly as she could without squeezing all the air out of her. Darlene was a tiny thing, but Beverly was desperate for a hug herself.

"Hey, mom. Let me come in and see how you are doing?"

Darlene knew something was wrong the minute she saw her daughter. She knew Beverly better than Beverly did. She still cursed herself for the times she did not interfere with Jack and his overzealous way of how he disciplined her. Her mind reeled at those dreadful memories that came flooding back before Beverly even let go of her.

Jack was screaming at Darlene. "Where is she? Why isn't she home yet? Doesn't she know that if she misses her curfew one more time I'm going to ground her for a month?"

Darlene had tried to calm him down, "Jack, honey, come here and finish the nightly news with me. She'll be home in just a little bit, I'm sure. She's on a double date and sometimes that can cause you to get behind when you have to drop off the other couple, you know."

Jack refused to listen to Darlene's rant on trying to placate him about his daughter's whereabouts. She was always making excuses for that girl.

The front door opened slowly, cautiously and Beverly tip-toed in praying her parents had already gone to bed. The minute she heard the television on her heart sank. This was not going to go well she knew.

Jack took three long strides and met Beverly as she closed the door gently praying her father did not hear her come in, but it was too late.

"Where the hell were you, young lady?' he bellowed. It's almost midnight and your curfew is 11 o'clock or had you forgotten that detail?"

Beverly's hands began to shake. She knew once her father started on her like this he would not calm down. Darlene shuffled into the hallway hoping to ease the situation, but it was not going to happen.

"Jack, let the girl come in and change her clothes. It's late and ...."

"Shut up, woman! If our girl is becoming the slut of the neighborhood well, she just better realize it now."

Beverly stuck her chin up in defiance and with all her young teenage pride and courage she blurted, "I am not a slut and don't you ever call me that!"

Jack's beady dark eyes bulged and the veins in his neck looked like they were going to pop. "All those boys want from you is to get into your vajayjay! I've told you that a hundred million times but, no, you don't believe me. In your vajajay, that's all any boy wants. And yes, you will become a slut at the rate you're going!"

Jack automatically raised his hand and swung down hard ready to slap Beverly, but before his pudgy palm landed, Beverly ducked and she felt the whoosh of air swirl around the top of her head.

Beverly's eyes squinted at her father. How many more times would she allow him to abuse her like this?

With a courage she did not know she possessed, Beverly shoved her father in his chest and spit out, "I'm not your whipping girl you can hit whenever you are pissed off at the world because you hate your life! I'll be outta here one day soon and then you'll be sorry you ever treated me this way."

Jack, who had almost tripped over the hallway table when Beverly pushed him, stood with his mouth open and his eyes glaring at her as he was leaning against the wall for balance. He wasn't sure whether he wanted to tangle with her at that moment, but he knew he would deal with her later.

Beverly, her fists clenched, sidestepped her father and ran to her room. She knew if she stayed in front of him any longer his slaps and punches would only start up again and finally hit the mark, and she was savvy enough to know his temper was not going to calm down soon.

Beverly left her father standing there flummoxed over that scuffle. He never tried to slap her again, but the memories of being subjected to his bouts of physical anger left her with emotional bruises long after the swelling and contusions healed.

• • •

Beverly followed her mom into the house and collapsed on the living room couch.

"Mom, we…I… have to talk. I have a lot of things I need to share with you and Mom, it's not good.

Darlene escaped into the kitchen for just a few minutes only to return with two wine glasses and a chilled bottle. She handed Beverly a glass, put her own on the table, and twisted off the cap of the wine.

Beverly held her glass up as her mother poured her a large helping of wine. Beverly took a long drink as if summoning up the courage to go on. She held onto her glass of wine while she poured her heart out to her mother. She needed that. She needed to trust someone who loved her unconditionally even though she knew there were some things she was sharing that were not completely ethical.

It felt good to release it all. Good, but she knew it wasn't right. She had let her jealousy, her anger, and her frustration with her personal life let alone her professional life lead her down a very slippery slope. A slope she had utterly fallen into and had no way of ever climbing out of it.

Darlene asked gently, "Are you sure, honey, that this teacher, this Carl in fact did something inappropriate? Because if you are not exactly sure, not 100% absolute,

I mean this is his future, his career, his livelihood. And whoever you told must have been able to corroborate what you said, right?"

Beverly took another long sip, swirled the velvety liquid in her mouth. She hesitated answering her mother. Her cheeks were flushed, and her head was spinning just a bit. She brushed her fingers through her dark hair, tugging on the ends as if the longer she held on to her strands, the easier she would find an answer.

"I don't know, Mom. I just don't know, but he has to have done something, or else the kids wouldn't call him a weirdo. I mean, what else could that mean? You know? And I had to tell the assistant principal. I had to. It's my civic duty to let someone know. What do they say, 'see something, say something? So I damned well did."

Darlene shrugged. "Kids say a whole lot of nothing, baby girl, and before you go accusing someone you gotta make sure. Really make sure. Did any of the students confide in you? Did anyone actually say to your face that this teacher, this particular teacher touched him or her or said something that gave that student the creeps? You know if you see something, yes, you have to say something. But, and that's the million-dollar question here, did you see something?

"Afterall, I would imagine that someone along the way would have opened up maybe to a counselor or the school nurse or another teacher."

"I know, Mom, I know," Beverly twisted in her chair

trying to get comfortable. The more her mother questioned her the more her body seemed to stiffen and cramp.

"So," responded Darlene, "Where is this teacher now? Is he still teaching in the same building as you?"

"Ummmm," Beverly started and stopped. "Well, as far as I know, he has been suspended. I don't know what the procedure is at this point, but I guess someone will investigate and if anyone comes forward then I'm pretty sure he will be terminated and that will be all. And if he is found guilty then he deserves what he gets. I can't stand it when men get away with hurting other innocent people."

Darlene stared long and hard at her daughter. She could tell how uncomfortable Beverly was acting and to her that was a sure sign that this entire conversation was meant for Beverly to somehow get validation for the actions she had taken.

"Beverly, baby."

"Hmmmm, yeah, Mom."

"Well, I was thinking, are we really talking about this teacher or are you somehow blending some of this about Ted and maybe even your father?"

CHAPTER 30

Carl and Chip walked into the hospital together. It had been a long time since the two brothers had ever walked side by side and there was a strong and positive electricity between them that had never existed before.

Chip gently pushed open the door to Leila DeWitt's room and entered, followed by Carl. Leila gradually opened her eyes and to her astonishment she saw both her sons standing by her bedside.

Leila chuckled. "Am I dead? Can this be happening?"

Chip smiled. "Easy there, big girl. Here, let's have you sit up a bit so you can talk to both of us more comfortably." Chip pulled on the lever and watched as Leila, with the widest grin on her face, kept staring at her two sons.

"Well, I'll be damned if I'm not sitting up in heaven looking at the best sight a mother can have. Chip, how the hell were you able to drag Carl down here with you, and by the looks of it you both are not trying to beat the crap out of each other."

Carl and Chip each grabbed one of the plastic chairs in the room and sat down, one on each side of her so they could each hold a hand.

Leila, sobbing uncontrollably, still kept the widest smile she ever had in her life.

Carl stood up, his hand never letting go of hers, "Now, Ma, c'mon. It's all good. I don't want you to cry. Chip and I have been talking and well, we sorta got our lives figured out. We are here to help you, Ma. Now, please, stop with the tears because you're gonna make me cry and that's just downright embarrassing."

Chip laughed. "Yeah, you don't want that nurse coming in here and yelling at me again. She practically threw me out of the room because she thought I was feeding you McDonald's!"

Leila laughed and rubbed her chestnut-brown eyes. Her cheeks were sunken in and her lips were very dry, but Chip noticed that the respiratory machine that was in her room the night before was nowhere in sight.

Carl thought his mother had aged overnight. A sudden intense pang of guilt for not coming to see her more often washed over him and he was heartbroken. He always used schoolwork as an excuse, but honestly, since he had not been in school for the last few months, he had no concrete reason to have avoided visiting her. His shame transferred to his cheeks which were now hot and red, and his own dark brown eyes (like his mother's) were starting to fill up with new tears. He was too humiliated to let her know why he wasn't working and therefore he had gone into his own personal hibernation.

Chip broke the awkward silence. "So, tell me, Mother dear, what has the doctor told you lately? I haven't talked to Dad today. What's the scoop and when can you go home?"

"Well," began Leila, very slowly and deliberately. "It seems that I have been having a series of TIA's. What did the doctor say that was again, Chip?"

"Mom, the doctor called them Transient Ischemic Attacks. You were very lucky cause Dad got you to the emergency room in time before you had a real heart attack."

Leila was breathing sluggishly but carefully, "Yes, dear, that's right. The doctor is watching me closely now, but he says I might be able to leave in a few days."

Chip looked at Carl and explained, "Mom was watching Emma for me when suddenly her arm went numb, and she started slurring her talk. Emma got hysterical when Granny couldn't pick her up, and it was Emma's screaming that alerted Dad. Dad came running into the kitchen, saw Mom, and immediately called 911. So, our Emma saved the day!!

"We need to find out what caused this problem and what we have to do to make sure Mom does not have another attack like this."

Carl nodded, appreciating the quick explanation. "What can I do to help?"

Chip's shoulders relaxed and he sighed. "Oh, Carl, you don't know how long I've waited to hear you say that to me! I've already taken off too much time at Dick's and I have a paper due for my class…"

Carl interrupted, "A paper due? What do you mean?"

Chip looked at his mother who would not stop smiling and her eyes now twinkled with delight. "You see, besides working at Dick's part time, I went back to college to get my teaching degree. It's taking a while, but I am at the very end of all the coursework. I can't afford to keep putting Emma with the babysitter and while dad does help now and then, he is going to have to take care of mom for a while. So…..do you think you could stay at my house for a week or so to take care of Emma until mom and dad have their routine set and they can help out? That is…" Chip looked at his mother and stroked her arm as he said, "That is, Mom, until you are able to be on your own two feet again!"

Leila squeezed both her sons' hands at the same time. "I will do everything in my power to get better so I can take care of my grandbaby again! You both just watch me!"

The room was silent, the air heavy with anticipation. Carl looked at his mother and then back at Chip and said, "Chip, I would love nothing better than to stay here and take care of my niece while you take care of your school-work and your job. I'm here for you, bro. And I have waited my whole life to say that to you!"

CHAPTER 31

Riley sat in her kitchen waiting for Cindy to come back down. Cindy was a handful, but Riley liked the challenge. The kitchen was shiny and clean and Riley looked around to see what ingredients she would need to make some pancakes. Before she started gathering the items, Riley had a thought.

She picked up her cell phone and opened a group message she had created. She closed her eyes while mentally creating her message, nodded to herself, and began clicking away:

Hey, group. Break is almost over. To celebrate lots of things I'm cooking up a huge pancake breakfast with all the extras included. If you want to join me, get over to my house within the hour or the food will be gone. I cook as good AF so you better get here soon!

Just as soon as Riley placed her cell on the counter, Cindy meandered into the room.

"Hey, Cin…everything okay up there? I mean is the room good? You comfy and all?"

Cindy was already overwhelmed by the luxury of the guest bedroom and now entering the kitchen with the expensive state-of-the-art equipment, Cindy was dumbstruck. She looked at names that she had never heard of before: Wolf and a Sub-Zero. Cindy thought how lucky she and her mom were to have GE appliances. Riley's kitchen, no, thought Cindy to herself, the entire house should have been in a magazine.

"Yeah," Cindy stammered. "The room is gorgeous. You know it's like the pictures I see in the magazines at the doctor's office. Riley, everything in your house is like a picture. You are really lucky."

Riley shrugged. "I guess so. But ya know, Cindy, things are great and all, but they are just things. Like I'd give anything to sit around every night and have dinner with my mom like you do. Or go to the mall or just sit and talk. Like they say, the grass isn't always greener on the other side; it just kinda looks like it."

Cindy went over to the sink and washed her hands. "Yeah, my therapist tells me the same thing. But I wouldn't mind trying the other grass just one time anyway."

Cindy stared at Riley while she grabbed tools and pans and bowls as though she were born in the kitchen. "Gosh, Riley, you really know what you're doing in here, don't ya?"

Riley smiled. It was nice being recognized for doing

what she absolutely loved. "Nah, I just look like I know what I'm doing." Riley started laughing and reached over and grabbed Cindy.

"C'mon, girlfriend, start earning your keep here, okay? Here's a wooden spoon. We stir with this thing, got it? And here's a bowl I filled with some pancake mix and some eggs and oil. Now you gotta blend. No, wait, easy there, Sherlock, I said stir not mix like you're on steroids!"

Cindy blushed. She loved being with Riley and having these back-and-forth conversations. It was natural and non-threatening, and Cindy felt so comfortable she never got anxious. I wish I could live here forever, she thought, almost jealous of the casual lifestyle Riley lived while surrounded by all the wealth that Riley took for granted. But Riley never name dropped or made her feel less than equal to her and for that, she was silently grateful.

Riley turned on her Spotify to the latest hits. She didn't ask Cindy if she had Spotify; Riley knew Cindy could not afford that luxury, but she made sure Cindy felt comfortable singing along with Beyonce and Ariana Grande.

"Hmmmm," Riley mumbled, "You have a very nice singing voice. Why don't you go out for chorus?"

"Really? You think so? No one ever told me that. I just love singing, but I am too shy to sing in front of anyone."

Riley snorted and brushed back a clump of hair from her eyes, "You know, you gotta have a 'I don't give a damn what others think about me' attitude or you'll never try anything."

Cindy nodded just as the front doorbell started clanging.

Riley was bent over the open oven door sliding in some homemade biscuits she wanted to bake when she shouted, "Come on in, the door's open!"

The front door flung open and in bounced Lucas, Mateo, Max, Jáquan, Jilly, Linette, and Shaynee.

Riley closed the oven door, wiped her hands on her pants and called out, "Hey, everyone, we're in the kitchen!"

Riley stared at Linette with her cropped hair. "Wow, girl, that's a new look!"

Linette smiled, her white teeth almost reflecting her new outlook. "And, would all of you call me Lane from now on?"

Cindy was confused but nodded her head up and down till her glasses almost bounced off.

Riley grabbed the metal bowl filled with pancake mix before Cindy dropped it and told Cindy to start handing out plates and silverware to everyone as chairs were pulled out and the infectious peals of laughter filled the room.

It seemed as though the entire group was talking all at once and Cindy could not help staring at them. Her eyes could not stop shifting from one person to the next as if she were an alien who had just been dropped onto the planet and had to identify this new species of humans. She loved the interactions and even if she wasn't one of them talking, she loved being a part of the group.

Riley plopped the hot pancakes on one large platter and handed it to Cindy while nodding her head in silent direction of the table. The kitchen table was large enough to seat each and every one and Riley loved seeing so many friends in her kitchen at one time. This never happened and she was embracing the warmth, the companionship, and the craziness of it all at once.

The multiple conversations were overlapping one another from Lane's new identity and haircut to their emails they had all sent to their principal to what they got for holiday gifts to frustration at how quickly their break was ending to how incredibly delicious Riley's pancakes were.

Riley kept the food coming. She whipped up a huge batch of eggs, along with the baked biscuits and some bacon that was already cooked and just needed reheating. She grabbed some various juices from the fridge along with several bottles of cold Starbucks that were overloaded with cream and sugar.

Jilly stopped eating for a second and shouted, "Hey, gang. Let's thank Riley for not only feeding us this incredible buffet of food but remember it was Riley who got us together to write to Dr. Libertino. Here's hoping we get to see our favorite teacher, Mr. DeWitt, back at school very soon." At this point, Jilly lifted her glass of orange juice and said, "Let's toast to all the good things we have today and hope for only good things in our future."

With shouts of "Hear, hear" and "Yeah, that's a cool toast" to "Hell, yeah!" everyone raised their glass of whatever they were drinking in their appreciation for Jilly's toast and Riley's hospitality.

The sounds of chewing, swallowing, burping, and laughter filled the cozy warm kitchen. Riley looked around and felt her stomach tingle with an odd sense of satisfaction from feeding so many friends and witnessing how much they were enjoying her culinary skills. This is what I want to do with the rest of my life, she thought to herself and with that knowledge she burst into peals of giggles that she never knew she possessed.

Looking around the large table that was quickly showing signs of empty plates and glasses, Riley exclaimed, "Well, you all made short work of my project, huh?"

With nods and grunts all around, there was a sudden hush that came over the group. Lucas stood up and whipped open his backpack that was hung over the chair. He pulled out a large bottle and unscrewed the cap.

"I think we ought to continue our breakfast party with a celebration to always remember. Mateo, did you bring what I asked you to?"

Mateo immediately stood up and grabbed his backpack and pulled out a large 2-liter bottle of Coke. "As you commanded, bro."

"What the hell are you doing?" demanded Riley. "Do you want to get me permanently grounded for having alcohol?"

Lucas shrugged as he began to pour small amounts into everyone's cup. Lucas looked over at Mateo and gave him the nod and Mateo immediately added a touch of Coke to each cup.

Lucas looked at Riley and smiled, his blue eyes twinkling mischievously, "Awww, c'mon, Mad Dog, it's only a little rum and coke. My mom will never know it's missing. And besides, it ain't gonna hurt anyone. I swear."

The group looked up at Riley waiting for her permission. *Damn, she thought, if this isn't the definition of pure peer pressure, I don't know what is.* And without another thought, her throat tight and her heart doing flip flops in her chest she choked out, "Oh, fuck it, drink up one and all and down the hatch as they say, at least I think that's what they say!"

CHAPTER 32

Antoine Saper hit his FaceTime icon on his cell phone. In a few seconds, the beautiful heart-shaped face of his sister filled his screen.

"Hey, big sister, how ya doin'?"

Alisa laughed. She had not laughed in a long time, and it felt good. She loved her younger brother Antoine and had not spoken with him in too many weeks. He was so often her confidante, her one true person whom she could always confide in no matter what the topic. But with the recent Beverly drama encompassing her daily breathing, she had sacrificed her numerous chats with Antoine.

"I've been better, little brother, been better, but now that I see your ugly face, well, I'm just heartbroken for those girls you keep tossing aside."

Antoine let out a long and hearty laugh, his deep brown eyes filled with love for his sister. His hair had been cut very short recently and the new look took Alisa by surprise.

"Uhhhh, little man, where are those gorgeous long Dreadlocks that I love?"

"Well, I was meaning to tell you sooner, but I've been so busy and, well, I've been accepted into the police academy and the first thing I needed to do was go high and tight. So there it is.

"Yes, ma'am, you are looking at a brand-new recruit and my class starts next week."

Alisa's eyes were glistening. "Oh, Antoine! I am so proud of you! How did Mama take it? I mean, a police officer! Wow!"

"Oh, she is very proud of me, and you know how I can tell? Cause every morning she is up before me, making me breakfast and hugging me before I even have the chance to leave the house! You know, I can't take much more of all this loving she is throwing on me!"

Alisa laughed. "You know Mama always loved you best. And this here just proves it!"

Suddenly, the laughter and joking seemed to fade away as Antoine's face took on a serious look.

"Uh, Sis, I need you to know something, I mean, I love you and I do need to call you more often, although the next few months I'm gonna be very busy. But I needed to let you know that, well, remember your friend, Janice?"

Alisa stared at Antoine. She hadn't thought about her old best friend in years. Between teaching and taking extra classes to get her master's degree, she barely called her mother to say hello let alone any other friends from her past. And now, especially with all the drama with Beverly, well, she felt totally out of touch with many things.

Alisa sucked in the air. "Tell me, what's going on? Don't beat around the bush now, Antoine, just say it right out."

"Okay, okay. Well, I saw Janice in the store the other day as I was getting some groceries for Mama. You know she's been feeding me so much lately…"

"Antoine! Tell me! Tell me now!"

"Sorry, A. When I saw Janice, and she looked good, whew, I mean she looked really good and…"

Alisa whistled into the phone, "Now, boy!"

"Okay, well, she told me to tell you that her mother passed away last month. And she…"

Alisa gasped. "Mama Billing? Oh, no!" Regret, sadness, guilt – they filled her heart like a broken dam gushing through her and drowning her. Memories flooded her senses as she remembered all the days playing with her childhood friend and helping Janice's mother in the kitchen. Afterall, it was Mama Billing who inspired her to follow her passion for food.

"Antoine. Antoine. What did she die from? I never knew she was sick. No, that's not fair. I haven't kept up with Janice in years so why would I even know if she was sick."

"Janice told me that her mama had some kind of blood disease; I don't know the name, and well, it finally took its toll on her.

"But, A., she wanted me to give you a message."

Alisa stared at Antoine. He had grown up so much in her eyes, she felt like she was speaking to a stranger. A good-looking man, but a man and not her baby brother.

"What's the message, Antoine?"

"She just said, 'Tell Alisa to call me, please. Tell her I need to talk with her.' And then she gave me her number."

"Go ahead, Antoine. Text me the number so I can call her. And tell Mama I will come visit this week before I have to go back to work. Tell her, Antoine. Don't forget now, cause if you do, I am still your big sister and I can whoop your ass any time I want to! You hear me?"

Antoine laughed, threw her a kiss, and clicked off.

Alisa waited a moment and then saw her phone notify her that a message had come through.

She opened the text from her brother and touched the cell number he just shared with her.

She listened to the phone ring and as soon as the voice on the other end said, 'Hello?' Alisa started crying.

"Janice? It's me, Alisa. Oh, girlfriend. I am so sorry about your mama, and I am so sorry you and I haven't talked in so long, and…"

Janice interrupted her. "Alisa? Oh, I am so glad you called. Can you come visit me? Now?"

Alisa was nodding her head up and down so hard she didn't realize that Janice could not see her.

She laughed through her tears but managed to choke out the words, "Oh, good God, Janice. I miss you so much. I am leaving first thing in the morning to come see you!"

CHAPTER 33

Barbara stared at her computer screen. Her small, dark chocolate-brown eyes glazed and watered so she closed them. Her hand gently removed her heavy glasses from her face. Her shoulders slumped, her neck tilted forward, and her pointy chin almost banged into her chest. She was exhausted mentally, emotionally, and now physically. She needed this time off to reenergize, but instead, she could not turn off what happened on the last day before she left work.

"Ms. Atkinson? Beverly lied. She lied about Carl. She lied about him being inappropriate. She lied about everything, and I feel like it's my fault for not coming to you sooner."

Barbara kept hearing Alisa's words over and over in her head. And then when she walked Alisa out to her car and reassured her that she had done the right thing, Barbara felt the air slip out of her like a leaky balloon. Walking back to the building, Barbara prepared for her meeting with her security team leader, Scott Sheldrake.

Scott entered Barbara's office just a few minutes after receiving her call. Barbara was always calling him for something regarding a student, but school was long over, the kids were all home somewhere and the entire staff had vacated the building as well. In fact, he was closing out his emails and about to lock up when Ms. Atkinson's secretary radioed him.

Scott could tell that something was very off the second he entered Barbara's office. Normally, her desk was extremely organized, almost OCD clutter-less, her bookshelves arranged in some magical order that she created, and her blinds arranged in perfect symmetrical fashion – each hanging slat was at a perfect 90-degree angle and matched the one next to it so it looked like one huge horizontal plank. But right now, the room was askew as though Barbara, or some alien, had flown in and touched every item and artifact in the room and tilted it. Barbara herself looked bent.

"Uhhh, hey, Ms. Atkinson," Scott coughed to get her attention and then spoke. He was a bit alarmed at seeing Barbara sitting at her desk, her glasses tossed haphazardly on her desk and her hands cupping her eyes as though she had been crying and did not want anyone to see.

Barbara took her hands away from her face when Scott spoke and stared at him for a moment as if she had completely forgotten why he was standing in her doorway, hesitant to come any closer.

Finally, breathing in the air for some magical strength she whispered, her voice wearisome and exhausted, "Thank you for coming to see me, Mr. Sheldrake. Please, close my door and come sit down."

Scott's eyebrows raised in his forehead and his mouth slid open in an O but he did not utter a sound. He gently closed her door and carefully took a seat. His years as a police officer had automatically placed his brain on full alert and he could tell this was not a social visit. He waited for Barbara to begin. This was her call; he knew she needed time to put her thoughts in order. And disorder was exactly what the room looked like. At first, he thought maybe she called him down to say someone had come into her room and attempted to vandalize it, but the hairs on his arm had raised and the back of his neck felt damp while his intuition knew a serious situation which he was now fully immersed in.

"Scottie," Barbara started, dropping the informal use of his last name. "Why didn't you tell me that Beverly Winewrought spit on you recently?"

Scott sat up in the chair and his shoulders squared back. He gulped. "I...I...well, I didn't think it was necessary. I..well..."

Barbara interrupted him, "You didn't think it was necessary?! An employee spat on you, and you didn't think that was important to alert me? What were you thinking? That she was having a bad day?"

Scott narrowed his eyes and glared at Barbara. He did not like someone telling him what to think or how to think. He had been in charge of too many police officers in his day and had to make thousands of decisions in his time from arrests to shootings and physical altercations too numerous to count. He dealt with sexual cases with juveniles that still stole into his dreams for not being able to solve certain investigations; he arrested hundreds of deranged and evil criminals and saw them enter the penal institution. Being spit on was way down on the list of high-priority scenarios.

"No, Ms. Atkinson, being spat on was disgusting and rude and totally off the professional bar, but running to tell you about that confrontation was not on my list of things to do. I was going to deal with Mrs. Winewrought the day staff returned to school. I needed to give her time to cool off."

"Well, Scott, it's going to be rather difficult to deal with Mrs. Winewrought and the spitting incident when we get back here because her issues are much more egregious than some saliva being flung at you."

Barbara was afraid to stop and take a breath because if she did she felt she would break down emotionally in front of Scott, and she refused to show that weakness. Instead, she sat up as tall as she could and stated rather detachedly, "Alisa Saper came to see me today."

Scott's two large, calloused hands rested on his knees. He was afraid that there was more to Beverly spitting on him than he let on and now he knew he was going to learn the ugly truth whether he wanted to or not.

Barbara stood up. She could not stay seated anymore. Her room was in such disarray it was causing her to feel dizzy. She turned her back on Scott and immediately began organizing the books and picture frames on her shelves. It seemed to soothe her and the more she glided around her office and tidied up, the more relaxed she appeared to be. Her entire body seemed to soften, and the words flowed smoothly. The act of straightening up her room created a logical, normal pattern that allowed her mind to formulate clear and unemotional thoughts.

"Alisa Saper," she repeated as though she needed to start again as she continued to walk around her room mechanically readjusting things. "Alisa was quite upset when she came by this afternoon. She felt she had to unleash the events of the past few months. The last few months, as you know, have all centered around Carl DeWitt and his investigation."

Scott's head jerked up at the point when Barbara mentioned Carl.

"What about Carl? Did Alisa know something? Had she spoken to him? Have you spoken to Carl, too?"

"Oh, Scott," Barbara released a huge sigh and continued, "Scott, I have to tell you because you need to know and I need to tell someone right now or I am going to lose my shit. Sorry. I apologize for that outburst. Scott, Beverly Winewrought made up the entire story about Carl and any inappropriate behaviors she alleged took place. Everything she said about Carl was an out-and-out lie and, Scott, we have sent that poor young man into hell for nothing."

CHAPTER 34

The kitchen was a mess. Even a wicked storm thundering through would not have left such complete and utter destruction. Half-eaten pancakes and runny eggs plastered onto cold plates teetered near the edge of the sink. A few dishes landed haphazardly in the bottom of the sink with dishwasher soap sloshing in the nooks and crannies of hardened food particles. Silverware was scattered on the countertops and some of them, still dripping with chilled pancake syrup, lay stuck to the ceramic tiled floor casting unearthly-like designs from an alien-scattered battlefield.

In the family room, Cindy sat cross-legged against the wall near the bookcase. She stared at her group of peers. What the hell happened, she thought to herself. Lucas lay prone with one leg perched up on the back side of the black suede couch. He was hiccupping out of control and giggling in between the loud and disgusting burps he ejected.

Jáquan had his face smashed in the expensive Oriental

rug, his dark curly locks spread out like the wings of a great fallen bird. Shaynee had her long legs resting on his back, her arms spread wide as though she was floating in the breeze, while she was singing Christmas carols with nonsensical words and very much off-key.

Linette/Lane was holding the kitchen broom as a dancing partner waltzing around the room, tripping every other step and trying to sing along with Shaynee. Mateo was playing some video game Cindy did not recognize but he kept getting killed so he screamed curses at the game and punched restart over and over again.

Cindy was scared. She had never been involved with a bunch of teens who were drinking alcohol. It frightened her because she did not know what to do. Her heart was racing, and her hands were clammy. She had taken one sip of whatever Lucas was passing around because she was too embarrassed to say no. So much for those 'Just Say No' posters that were plastered in the nurse's office as well as her health class.

"Oh, come on, Cindy pants," mocked Riley. "You're only taking a sip. What harm could it bring? Really, Cindy, you're being a baby! Look, we are all just having a small cup to celebrate. What are you so afraid of?"

Cindy had shrugged. Riley was right. What harm could come to just taking a sip? Besides, we were all together in the room, safe and warm. It's not like we were out driving or anything stupid like that.

Finally, Cindy accepted the cup. She brought it to her lips and slowly, very slowly, let the cool, silky potion that was tinged with bubbles slide down her throat. But once she swallowed, the smooth liquid burned the back of her throat so much she started coughing and could not stop. They all started laughing at her.

"Oooh," laughed Mateo. "Is this your first drink, little girl? It's alright, Cin, I gave you mostly coke anyways."

Linette/Lane jumped in. "C'mon, Cindy. Quick, take another slug and it won't be so bad. There you go. Good girl!"

Cindy put the cup down. "I'm okay. I'm okay. I just wasn't used to that brand, I guess. What I drink at home is much smoother. Okay?"

Lucas laughed and kept pouring his liquor into everyone's cup while Mateo kept adding warm Coke. In a few minutes, everyone was toasting and giggling and snorting snot uncontrollably causing more laughter and raucous pushing and grabbing.

Riley attempted to clean the mess left by everyone, but the more everyone kept drinking the sloppier the volume of the mess swelled as plates and silverware were shoved and haphazardly tossed and landed in various areas. Riley prayed that none of the dishes broke, but she realized she was too late for that wish.

Riley walked out of the kitchen muttering to herself that she would have plenty of time to clean up once everyone left. Besides, she thought, I can always make Cindy help me.

Jilly had clicked on YouTube on her phone and started

playing music while the others pretended to dance and move. Cindy decided to push herself into the corner of the room using the bookcase as her support and hid herself there while everyone else looked like drunken zombies lost in the woods gyrating awkwardly.

It did not take long for most of them to exhaust themselves. Lucas plummeted on the couch, Jáquan had face-planted on the rug with Shaynee on top of him and the others scattered around doing their own thing.

But where was Riley? Where was Jilly?

Cindy stood up slowly. The room was spinning, and she squeezed both her hands to her temples to steady herself. She heard whimpering and stumbled over Shaynee to follow the moaning cries.

The bathroom was around the side of the kitchen and Cindy plodded over there and then froze at the door. Riley was perched on the edge of the bathtub with both her hands yanking up Jilly's hair. Jilly was vomiting violently into the toilet bowl. She heard Riley sssshhhhhing her, but Jilly was crying and coughing and throwing up all at the same time.

"Holy shit!" yelped Cindy. "Oh, my God! Is she okay?"

Riley looked up shocked that anyone would have dared to enter the bathroom and witness the revolting scene taking place.

"Go away, Cindy!" barked Riley. "There's nothing you can do here. Don't make her feel worse than she already does."

At that point, Riley let go of Jilly's hair and reached

for the dampened towel that Riley had left soaking in the sink. She squeezed out the excess water and rubbed Jilly's neck and face with it.

"On second thought, Cindy. Do me a favor, would you? Go into the kitchen and grab me a ginger ale in the fridge and bring it back here. Go, go, go. Oh, no, she's gonna blow again." And then Riley threw the towel back in the sink, swiped the toilet handle to get the remaining putrid vomit down and out of the bowl, clutched Jilly's hair again, and said in as soothing a voice as she could muster, "Let it go, girl. Let it out. You'll feel better."

Cindy turned as fierce noxious pukings sloshed in the toilet water and the bitter smells of bile swirled in the air. Cindy, feeling sick to her stomach herself as vomiting always made her feel like hurling, tried breathing slowly and steadily. She made her way back through the family room and was not surprised to see that no one had moved since she left the room just a few minutes before.

"You are all going to regret that you did all that stupid drinking," admonished Cindy as she glared at everyone. "I can't believe this."

Cindy was about to turn into the kitchen when suddenly she heard the front door open and in walked Dr. Jeanine Maddox, Riley's mother.

Jeanine took one look at everyone, her eyes bulging open as wide as was humanly possible. Cindy, standing closest to her, opened her mouth to say something, but only gasped.

Dr. Maddox composed herself and looking at Cindy who seemed to be the only one who was functioning, uttered in a very controlled and commanding voice, "Where the hell is my daughter!?"

CHAPTER 35

Carl never realized how much joy he could feel until he spent the week watching his niece, Emma. She was a little version of Chip with her bouncing curly brown hair and her startling blue eyes. She was full of energy and curiosity and never ceased to amaze Carl.

"Uncca Carl," she questioned, her tiny eyebrows scrunched high in her forehead, "Why do you have to go home?"

Carl's voice skipped a beat as he caught his breath. He had fallen for his niece and the thought of him having to leave her left him feeling empty inside.

"Well, little rabbit," he murmured gently to her as she cuddled on his lap with her favorite book clutched in her tight tiny fists. "I do have to go back and get some things cleared up, but I will be back soon, I promise!"

She stared up at him, her eyes filled with love and wonder at this man who looked like her daddy except for his eyes and hair. "I love you, Uncca Carl. Don't go."

Carl hugged her and whispered gently, "I love you too,

bunny. How about we finish reading your book now, okay? Your grandpa and your daddy are coming home soon and then we are going to go visit grandma."

"Whee," exclaimed Emma. "Read! Read! Read!" Emma clapped her hands in joy as Carl quickly snatched her book before it tumbled to the ground.

The day flew by as Carl was able to read *The Very Hungry Caterpillar* three more times before Emma's yawning morphed into snoring as she dozed in his arms. Carl gently scooped her up and laid her in her new bed that was flushed with the floor just in case she rolled off the mattress. She was so proud that she did not sleep in a crib anymore, but Chip was uncomfortable with her so high up in a bed even with sidebars.

Carl slid the quilt over her curled body and wiped the curls from her face smiling at the way her thumb had found her mouth the minute he positioned her on the bed.

While Emma slept, Carl listened to his voice messages from Neva. He wanted so desperately to call her, but Lemont had told him not to contact anyone, no exceptions.

I am always the good guy, thought Carl, *and it sure hasn't paid off for me lately.* With a new rebellious attitude that shocked him, Carl listened to Neva's soothing voice one more time, only this time instead of closing the voice message, he hit the return call and held his breath.

Carl heard Neva's voice and almost choked up before he could talk.

"Hello, Neva?" Carl whispered so softly he wasn't sure Neva heard him, but she did.

"Carl? Oh, Carl, it is you!" Neva exclaimed. "I am so glad you called me back. I have been worrying about you for so long and I know I am not supposed to call you, but I couldn't take it any longer." Neva chuckled and said, "Besides, Atticus was concerned that you haven't been by in a while, so I knew I needed to check on you.

"Carl, how are you, dear?"

Carl took a cautious, long breath. "Neva, I am so sorry I haven't talked with you. I was told not to and, well, I am tired of listening to everyone else tell me what to do. I guess winter break is almost over."

Neva sighed, "Yes, it is. And everyone had been asking about you every day and no one knows why you aren't here and well, there are so many questions with no answers."

"Neva," Carl faltered for a moment and then he continued, "I honestly do not know what happened. I do not know why I was sent home or if someone said something about me. I am so confused and hurt and every day I keep thinking this nightmare is going to be over and then it's not.

"I am waiting for my representative to call me. I missed a meeting, but my mother is in the hospital. She was supposed to come home but she had another one of her mini-strokes, so they are keeping her at the hospital."

"Oh, Carl, I am so sorry. Is there anything I can do for you?"

"Gee, thanks, Neva. I truly appreciate that, but there has been some good coming out of this and I want to tell you all about it when I come back. You see I have been staying at my brother's place babysitting his little girl. Hah, I'm an uncle and I'm loving it!"

"Oh," cried Neva, tears gently sliding down her cheeks with joy. "I am so happy for you. Oh-oh, here comes Atticus to my rescue thinking I'm upset. No, baby boy, I'm okay."

Carl could tell she was rubbing Atticus and calming him down because he could hear Atticus whining in the background.

Just then the front door opened, and Chip walked in.

"Listen, Neva, my brother just returned home from work. We are going to go to the hospital to see my mother. I promise to call you tomorrow. Take care, and Neva, thank you for calling me." Carl hit his end button and looked up at Chip.

Chip smiled. He was enjoying his newfound relationship with his brother and especially the way Carl and his daughter had bonded.

"Listen, Carl," Chip began slowly, "Dad is coming over to watch Emma while you and I go to the hospital. The doctor called me and said he needed to talk with us as soon as possible."

Carl rose immediately, slipped his phone in his pocket, and grabbed his coat. The sound of a car door shutting shattered the quiet of the room as he recognized his father's car in the driveway.

Harry DeWitt entered the house, his shoulders slumped forward and his hat sitting somewhat cockeyed on his head. He looked tired, worn out. He wasn't used to being alone and with Leila in the hospital for over a week now, he was exhausted.

"Hey, Dad," both brothers said at the exact same time.

Chip continued, "Dad, Emma is asleep in her bed. Carl and I will go to the hospital and then when we come back you can go. Thanks for watching Emma for me again."

Harry smiled. He had done many things wrong in his marriage and with his boys, but seeing them together had given him new hope in his life.

"Go on," he said. "I got Emma. This grandpa knows all the tricks with her. And if you don't mind, we might be hitting the kid's meal at MickeyDee's if she wakes up and she's hungry. I hear they have a new toy this week!"

Carl walked over to his father. "You're the man, Dad! Thanks. We'll see you later, okay?"

Chip waved and said, "Thanks, Pop. For everything. We'll see you soon. Don't forget to put Emma in her car seat!"

Harry nodded and grunted, his lagging body already in the chair by the television.

There wasn't much conversation between Chip and Carl on the way to the hospital. They had talked and talked all week about so many things – from their childhood to their sister to their parents and everything in between. There was a new closeness between them and a tacit understanding that did not need small talk.

When they reached the room where their mother was, Carl sensed something amiss.

"Chip," he started, "Look at mom. She looks really pale.

I was hoping we could bring her home and it seems like she has had another setback."

Chip nodded and walked to the other side of the bed. He picked up his mother's frail hand and held it to his cheek.

Carl touched his mother's shoulder, and she slowly opened her eyes. Her voice was barely a whisper as she tried to speak, "Oh, my boys. Oh, my sons. I love you both so much. You make me so happy to see you together like this.

"I've wanted this for so long. Promise me you both will be together always, and that little Emma will have you both in your life. Promise me."

Carl reached for Leila's hand as both sons held onto their mother. Her body was cold and tiny under the hospital blanket, and her lips were cracked and dry as she talked.

"And promise me you will watch over your father. I know he hasn't been the best dad, but promise me…"

She stopped talking. Her eyes closed. Her face seemed to squeeze together as though she was suffering something awful, something the boys could not bear to watch.

Carl spoke first, "Mom. We love you. Chip and I will be together, and we will make sure dad is okay."

Chip added, "And Emma is going to be just fine, mom. Together we are a family. Again. And we want you home with us."

Leila did not open her eyes, but one tear slowly slipped out of her eye and rolled down her sunken cheek. She smiled weakly, her cracked lips never opening. She took one last breath and then she was gone.

CHAPTER 36

Shaynee held a dish towel in her hand waiting for the next pan. Cindy finished scrubbing the pot and passed it to Shaynee. Cindy leaned her elbows, exhausted, her hands dripping with soap suds. Without thinking she pushed her bangs away from her eyes leaving globs of dissolved Dawn and crumbs clinging to her wet bangs.

Cindy moaned and looked over at Riley who was still wiping crumbs from the table. "Riley, are you going to get in tons of trouble?"

"Nah," Riley said softly. "My mom is really angry, but we'll work it out. Besides, you're here hanging out with me so she can't blow her gasket right away. Shaynee, here you go, girl, hand me that pot so I can hang it up. Thanks."

Shaynee sighed. "Hey, I'm sorry I'm still here, Riley. My mom works pretty far from home, and I guess she is not hurrying to come get me. We haven't been on good terms lately, anyway."

Riley shrugged and her deep amber eyes twinkled.

"Look, don't apologize. It's cool. My mom, being the mom and doctor she is, would never let anyone go home half-cocked like everyone was. She was pissed off, but she'll deal."

Shaynee picked up her water bottle and took a long swig. "Thanks for the Excedrin. My head is kicking me from here till next Tuesday and I'm never, ever gonna drink that crap again."

Cindy joined in. "Me neither and I only took a small sip."

Riley chuckled. "Yeah, Cindy, we all know how much you drank."

Cindy stuck her hands back in the soapy water and with a small 'hmmmmppph' continued washing in silence.

Shaynee laughed, "Oh, Cindy, we were all here together and that was the cool part. Hah, I bet no one is going to believe us when we go back to school. And speaking of going back to school, uh, do we call Linette Lane from now on and like, uh, is she going to go into the girls' bathroom with us or the boys? I'm so confused?"

Just at that moment, Jeanine Maddox walked into the kitchen.

"Listen, girls, I want to thank you for cleaning up with Riley, although if it were up to me, I would make my daughter clean the ENTIRE kitchen by herself! Wouldn't I, Riley?"

Riley glared at her mother. She was embarrassed that her mom made each one of her friends call their mothers or fathers to come pick them up. She refused to let any of them walk home by themselves. And each one had to explain in detail why they were being picked up.

Jeanine continued, "And poor Jilly, that girl finally stopped throwing up. She is going to have one very bad headache tonight. And speaking of tonight... Cindy, I hope you know you are still staying with us. Baby, you are staying with us as long as you need to so do not feel bad that we did not call your mom."

Cindy choked on her saliva and could hardly stop coughing. Riley leaned over and slapped her on her back until she stopped. "It's okay, Dr. Maddox, my mom would have understood, but right now I don't know what she's thinking about or anything."

"Cindy," Jeanine said soothingly, "later tonight you and I are going to have a good talk about what your mom is going through. And Riley and I will be with you every step of the way. Okay?"

Cindy nodded. Words would not come out of her mouth right now and tears were threatening to flow so she bit her lower lip and attempted to smile.

The doorbell rang and Shaynee jumped, her long curls falling in her face. "Oh, damn, it must be my mother. Thanks, Dr. Maddox, for everything. And, hey, Riley, I'll see you in school. You too, Cindy." Shaynee grabbed her bookbag, her jacket and ran to open the door.

Mrs. Moulder stood there with a large frown on her face. Her hazel eyes and blonde hair were in direct contradiction to Shaynee's light brown eyes and dark hair. "Shaynee, we have some talking to do, young lady!" Seeing Jeanine,

Berkley Moulder stretched out her arm and grasped her on the shoulder. "Oh, I am so sorry we have to meet under these circumstances. I promise you this will never happen again. You have my word."

Jeanine smiled. Every mom who came to pick up their child had the same conversation. "It's okay. I'm glad they were here together and not out joyriding or putting themselves in any other serious forms of danger. I would never allow them to go home without the parents knowing what took place here and since I was not here when this ill-conceived party occurred, believe me when I tell you my daughter will not be entertaining for a long time to come!"

Berkley nodded in agreement. "Come on, Shaynee. You have a ton of chores to do when you get home. And your brothers, well, I'll tell you more about your babysitting when we are in the car.

Shaynee was embarrassed and humiliated. She saw how Riley and her mom stared at her mother who looked so physically different from her, and even though this was not the appropriate time she decided to blurt out, "Really, Mom, and then after that you can explain to me why I look so different from you and dad! And this time I have real proof! And we need to talk about this, okay?"

Berkley looked like she had been slapped by a tree limb that had fallen smack into her face. She turned bright red, then purple. She grabbed Shaynee by her arm and yanked her out the door and without turning around shouted, "Thank you again and good day!"

Riley quickly went to the door and shut it gently. She

leaned on the closed door and whistled. "Wow, what a day this has been!"

Jeanine cracked a smile as she said, "Oh, my dear. This day has only just begun for you!"

Riley's eyes turned into brown slits and her mouth opened wide.

CHAPTER 37

Alisa's hand reached up to knock at the large door of her childhood friend, but before she touched the bright red painted wood Janice flung it open and grabbed Alisa in a huge bear hug.

"Oh, my God, is it really you?" squealed Janice as she could not stop hugging Alisa.

Alisa tried to suck in the air that had just been squeezed out of her as she laughed and cried at the same time. "Yes, you goof, it's me! Let me look at you!"

The two women parted for a second before Janice jumped up and down shouting, "Oh, do come in! Come in out of the cold and bring your suitcase and whatever else you have and…"

Alisa smiled from ear to ear. It was the old Janice. She never could stop talking as a little girl and now as an adult, oh, my, she was just as talkative as a locomotive rushing through the house.

Janice could not stop. "Look at you, Alisa Saper. It is still Saper, isn't it? No man has caught your eye and your heart and caused you to lose your breath and, wow, you are incredibly gorgeous! Look at your hair! I absolutely adore it! And…."

Alisa tried to jump in. "And look at you, Miz Janice Billing! Aren't you a picture to behold! And you have not gotten hitched either, have you? What happened to us that we have not found our Mr. Rights out there?"

Janice sighed. "Well, for starters, being a military brat, I never stayed in one place long enough to have a relationship. And now finally my dad retired and decided he wanted to go back and live in Texas, his true home state. Mom was visiting me here because I had just started my new job and she was so excited for me, and wait…" Janice's voice choked a little. "Let me get you settled in a bit, and I will go over everything with you. Plus, I want to hear all about you and what you are doing to inspire the youth of today in our kitchens. Oh, praise the Lord, my mom would be so very proud of you, Alisa girl."

It didn't take too long for Alisa to throw her belongings into the guest room, and change into some comfy yoga pants and a top only to find Janice in the living room with a tray filled with scrumptious charcuterie and a bottle of wine ready to be poured.

"Come, Alisa, my dear friend. We may not have our Barbies and our Ken dolls anymore, but we have each other and an awful lot to catch up on. So, let's fill our glasses and make a toast to an old friendship rekindled."

Alisa smiled, the first real smile she had felt for a long time. "Ohhh, Janice, it's so good to be with you. I have had such an up-and-down first semester and sadly, I really did not have a true friend to talk to about what has been happening to me.

"But before that, tell me, tell me please, what have you been doing and what has happened to Mamma Billing?"

Janice wiped a tear that had suddenly slid down her puffy red cheeks. It had been so long since she had told the story of her mother's demise and it was not easy for her. She could not just jump into it so instead, she took the long way around telling Alisa what she had been doing since they were little girls.

"You know," she began slowly, "being with a military dad was not always the easiest life. I mean, yeah, it was great to see other countries but going to all the DOD schools, well, that was not always fun."

Alisa interrupted, "Oh, jeez, I forget. What is a DOD school?"

Janice stopped and looked up at the ceiling, her cobalt blue eyes seemed miles away. She spoke almost mechanically as she explained, "The DOD schools are the Department of Defense schools that we military kids go to when our parents are deployed out of the country. Sometimes I got to go to a local school but more often than not, my dad insisted I stay at a DOD school.

"They were okay, just not always filled with the culture of the country and I longed to explore and go on adventures everywhere. We were stationed in Germany and then Spain and then South Korea for a bit. And yes, I collected trinkets wherever I went, but I collected things, not friends.

As soon as it was time for dad to pack up, we went into the backing away mode. In other words, say goodbye, not let's write and stay in touch because there would have been too many to keep up with so it was always natural to just say 'see ya sometime in our lives' and off we would go."

"But what about your brothers? Weren't they close with you?"

Janice shrugged. She clasped her hands together and reflected, "For a time being we were close, but because they were so much older than me, they were able to choose whatever college they wanted to go to and that left me pretty much as an only child."

"Oh," exclaimed Alisa. "I am so sorry," She reached for Janice's hands and held them tightly.

"Don't feel so bad for me, Alisa. It wasn't the worst scenario. I graduated high school and found a small college in the Rockies. I liked it. I majored in liberal arts, so I graduated with a degree in nothing specific, and so I struggled to find my calling. What did I want to do with my life?"

Alisa's deep coffee-colored eyes watered, and she took a long sip of her wine hoping to calm her emotions. It did not work. She realized she was crying and wasn't quite sure how to stop herself. She tried to help Janice focus.

"So, where are your brothers now?" she asked.

"Oh, they are both married, working in DC for the government and they have two children each, so I am the spinster aunt who sends fantastic gifts for the holidays and their birthdays."

"Hey, I'm not married, and I don't consider myself a

spinster, friend. I am enjoying my single lifestyle and I'm here to make sure you see it that way, too."

Alisa reached for some cheese and sausage. She did not realize how hungry she was, and she was beginning to get a headache.

"I'm sorry, Alisa. I guess I'm feeling pretty depressed right now." Janice took a sip of her wine and grabbed some cheese and crackers.

"Janice," Alisa started slowly, "tell me about your mom. What happened?"

Janice leaned back on her couch and tucked her legs underneath and covered herself with an Afghan.

She picked up her blue throw pillow and hugged it tightly as though it would give her extra strength.

"Well, we had been living in this house, my mom and dad you see. And as soon as Dad decided he wanted to retire and buy a condo down south, well, Mom wasn't too happy. She wanted to be able to see her grandkids whenever she wanted to and moving farther south would only make it so that she could see them on holidays and probably less and less as they were getting older.

"Dad was adamant. He had gone down to search out the best condo he could find and was hoping Mom would fall in love with their newest home. He was so used to moving around that staying here was getting too old for him. He was getting his itches as I called them."

"Was your mom ill?"

Janice choked back tears. "That's just it, Alisa. She wasn't sick; she was in the best health she had ever been in. She was taking yoga classes and going to our local college for some computer training. She was having the time of her life."

Alisa urged Janice on. "Go ahead," she choked out in a whisper.

So, it's just my mom and me and she suddenly jumps up one night and says, "Oh, dear, I forgot to mail the birthday card to Bryson." Janice added, "That's my nephew; Mom's oldest grandson."

Janice continued, "So I told her I would take the letter in the morning, and she insists on going right there and then. She didn't want the card to arrive late. Unfortunately, Mom didn't have a car since Dad had it and she asked me to borrow mine.

"I explained to my mom that my car was new, and she hadn't driven it yet, but she was adamant so I told her to go ahead."

Janice stopped. She leaned forward and picked up her wine glass and the wine bottle and filled it again. She swallowed a long drink, put the glass down, and leaned back on the couch again.

"Mom drove my car down to the post office but they had closed for the day, so she drove around the neighborhood trying to find one of the stand-alone mailboxes. When she finally found it, she was so excited she jumped out of the car and ran over to the box, but...." Janice stopped talking and stared at the ceiling, closing her eyes as if to erase the memory.

"But what, Janice? What happened next?"

"Oh, Alisa. Mom never put the car in park; she mistakenly shifted the car into reverse when she jumped out and the car started to move slowly until it hit her and dragged her under the car as the car now kept going in circles while still in reverse. Mom never saw it coming. My only consolation is that the doctor told me she was killed instantly as her head hit the concrete from the collision. Oh, God, Alisa. She was run over by my God damned car. I should have never let her go alone. It's all my fault. It's all my fault."

Alisa quickly put her glass down, moved over to the couch, and held Janice in her arms. Janice's sobs were uncontrollable. Janice was shaking and crying and shouting that it was all her fault over and over again.

"Hush," said Alisa softly. "It's not your fault. It was never your fault. It was a freak accident. Shhhh, it's okay. I'm here now. And I know that your mom is watching over you and letting you know that it's okay."

The two women sat like that holding on to each other for what seemed like hours. Alisa's soothing voice was like a soft warm blanket to Janice, and she relaxed and uncurled her body. She turned to Alisa and breathed, "God, I'm a mess. I've got snot all over your shoulders and I feel like I want to vomit."

"Hey, the snot I can deal with, but no vomiting. Uhhh, nope – not gonna happen."

And then the two women smiled at each other and started laughing and giggling like they were six years old again.

CHAPTER 38

Carl was pulling into the driveway when his cell phone started buzzing. It was Lemont Jacobs, his union representative.

"Hello, Carl?" asked Lemont.

"Yes, hello, Lemont. How are you?" Carl wasn't friends with Lemont, but he respected their relationship that was forged on his being suspended from teaching.

"I am well, thanks for asking. I was hoping you would be available next week for an official meeting. And, also, I was very sorry to hear about your mother. I explained that situation to the assistant superintendent as I had to reschedule your meeting last week."

"I appreciate that, Lemont. I really do. It has been very exhausting and for me, well it was very sudden." Carl shut off the car and went into his father's home still holding onto his cell phone and his bags. He figured that his dad would not be coming back to the house for quite some time and Carl thought staying there might be therapeutic in some way.

"So, listen, Carl. Next week, and I'll get back to you with the exact time and everything, but for now, I'd like you to ask as many of your colleagues as you can to email me a letter of character reference for you. You know my email, so you will need to send that out to whoever you think will have the most positive comments about you. Got it? Now get busy, my man, because this is showtime, like the fourth quarter with no more time outs, like..."

"Okay, Lemont. I get it, man. And I appreciate all you have done for me. I will get those emails out to you as soon as I can. And Lemont?"

"Yeah, Carl?"

"Thanks, man. For everything."

"It's cool, Carl. I believe in you, I honestly do. Let's get this over with and get you back in the classroom because that is where you belong, my man! Take care, now." And with that, Lemont's call ended.

Carl grabbed his bookbag and his suitcase and headed upstairs into his old bedroom. At this point, he had a feeling this house was going to be his in a short time seeing how his father would be spending most of his time helping Chip with Emma.

The funeral for his mother was sweet and quiet and poignant. Carl and Chip both said a few words at the church service while his dad held onto Emma as though she were giving him the necessary strength to carry on.

But now Carl was all business. And after emptying his suitcase and throwing all his clothes in the washing machine he jumped into the shower and tried to cleanse his mind and his soul of the past few weeks. Learning about his beautiful and adorable niece Emma, reconnecting with his brother, making amends with his father, and holding his mother as she breathed her last breath on Earth, well, it felt like a lifetime all bottled up and he wanted to tuck it deep inside his heart forever. He needed to store it there for safekeeping and when his whole ordeal with the school system was over, he would take these past few months of incredulous events out again and let himself feel the entire range of emotions from joy to sadness to anger to fear. But not now. Now he had to stay on track, be focused and clear-headed with what he needed to accomplish in the next seven to ten days.

Drying his thick curly brown hair with his towel, Carl sat down on the couch and picked up his cell phone. He listened to Neva's messages for the umpteenth time, but now he pressed the blue icon to call her back. She answered immediately.

"Carl?" she asked nervously. "How are you, son? Are you okay? I've been so worried and waiting to hear back from you again, and...oh, my...I'm not even letting you answer. Please, go ahead, say something."

"Uhh, hello, Neva?"

Neva laughed long and hard. "Oh, goodness gracious it is so good to hear your voice."

Carl snickered and smiled. He knew she couldn't see him smiling but he knew she would sense it. Neva was so incredibly intuitive he felt she was part psychic.

"Neva," he began, "it's so good to hear your voice again.

I have missed you so much. Oh, and Atticus, too!" He could hear her chuckling and he continued.

"I have some things I need to share with you. I can do a little of that now. However, I still have a lot of holes that I truly do not know how to fill since I am pretty clueless about what has happened to me or the real reason why. All I know is that someone… someone, and I have no clue as to who, but someone has told the administration that I have been inappropriate with students to such an extreme degree that they had to suspend me immediately. Which, of course, you know they did.

"All this time that I have been home I was told I could not discuss my case with anyone or that person would be in violation of, gee, I have no clue what, but I gather something bad. At any rate, so many other things have happened in my life since I was suspended and I want to share them with you at another time and definitely in person, but for now, I have a huge, big, enormous favor to ask of you."

"Oh, Carl, whatever favor you need from me you've got it, my son."

"Neva, please understand if you are uncomfortable with what I am asking, you do not have to go through with this."

"Carl, are you asking me to marry you?" Neva laughed and the stress Carl felt totally vanished.

"Oh, God, how did you know?" Neva's laugh was always infectious, and Carl's entire body sank into the couch like a huge sack of sand that was cut open.

"Go on, Carl, my boy. Waddya got for me. I can handle it."

Carl went on to explain what Lemont wanted and said he would text her the email address. As soon as Neva replied, "Yes, a thousand times yes and then some. I will do it as soon as I get off the phone with you."

"And, Neva, do you think it's a good idea to ask Cassandra? I mean I haven't spoken to her since the day I left, but damn it all, we were just growing into such a nice relationship. You know, the going out to dinner sort of thing."

Neva sighed and said, "Carl, she thinks the world of you. Of course, she would be a wonderful person to ask. Trust me, she will! And now, let's put our heads together and help you with some other staff who you should ask. Scott Sheldrake for sure."

Carl and Neva spoke for almost an hour as they chatted and arrived at a healthy list of names for Carl to ask for character references.

For the first time in months, Carl felt confident in his life. "Neva, I cannot thank you enough for always being there for me. I know school starts up again and I won't be there, but I am hoping, oh, God, I am hoping I will return soon."

"Bless you, Carl. No one should have to go through what you have gone through. You're a great, compassionate teacher, a good human being, and a special friend. And don't you forget it! Now get a good night's sleep. I have some big-time writing to do."

And with that she clicked off. Carl smiled, pumped

his fist into the air, and shouted to the quiet room, "Hell, yeah!"

Carl quickly went through his contacts and began the process of calling everyone Neva and he agreed would be strong support for him, starting with, of course, Cassandra.

CHAPTER 39

Lucas slumped in the chair about as deeply as he could. He hated coming to see his therapist. She was nice and all, he thought, but he hated discussing his childhood and the horrible and embarrassing things that happened to him. Those disgusting things being the time his father attempted to touch him inappropriately.

"So, Lucas," Miss Anna began gently. She knew he was not embracing their conversations. They had only had three or four so far, but she felt that she had not broken through his tough exterior. His mother had shared with her about the drinking party at one of his friends during the break. He was grounded and according to Lucas, the drinking incident was no big deal.

"Yeah, I know what you are going to say to me," muttered Lucas, "Why did I bring a bottle of liquor to my friend's house?"

"Well," Anna said softly, "you are not of age to be drinking, but I am not here to judge you, right?"

"Aren't you?" questioned Lucas. "Isn't that the whole

purpose of me sitting here so you can tell me all the things I did wrong and why I did them and how I should love my stepfather unconditionally and forgive my mother for marrying him and forget the tiny fact that the father I had always loved and adored is a no-good sonofabitch pedophile? Isn't that the reason I'm sitting here, huh?"

"Whew," exclaimed Anna, "you said quite a mouthful there, my young man. And, no, my job is not to teach you right from wrong. You have always known that. My job, if you want to call it that, is to allow you to say whatever it is you want to share with me. Put the cards on the table so to speak.

"And, Lucas, whatever you do reveal to me is confidential. You know that, right?"

Lucas shifted his weight in his seat and combed his fingers through his curly hair as if he could find the answers to his problems somewhere in his thick locks. He sat there for what seemed like hours. Miss Anna relaxed in her seat, folded her hands in her lap, and allowed her soft hazel eyes to focus on the floor, waiting patiently. She knew he was like a soda can that had been shaken and then popped open only to spew out liquid over everything in sight. And so she sat. And sat. And waited.

He needed the time. He needed to feel her trust. He needed to let go of all the anger and hatred and fear and confusion that had been fermenting inside of him before he burst. And when was that explosion coming? She hoped he could release some of it with her. So Anna stared at her rug as if it held all the answers to his confused world.

Without lifting her eyes she could tell by his stirring in his seat that he was agitated and that the proverbial soda can was about to blow.

"Okay," he suddenly jolted up in his seat. "So tell me why I had to be born to a goddamned sicko for a father. I mean, I loved him. I wanted to be just like him! He was my whole world and then he destroyed it. And, I think," Lucas let out a sob, but he sucked it back in quickly and continued, "that's why I keep destroying things now.

"Yeah, it was me who wrote those stupid racist words in the locker room and on the side of the building. And, okay, shit, yeah, I keyed my teacher's car because she makes me feel like she understands me, but she can't. She doesn't get it and I hate her for being so nice to me even when I'm so shitty towards her."

Lucas didn't realize that he was talking so fast that spittle was spraying from his lips and his ocean blue eyes filled with overwhelming tears. He was embarrassed by his admissions and wanted to take it all back, but he could not.

Lucas slowed down, wiped the spit from his lips with the back of his hand, and then swiped the snot from his nose with his sleeve. He mumbled softly, "Why? Why does someone do something like that? He turned my whole world upside down in an instant. And then along comes this cop who saves me like some superhero from a Marvel movie and my mother falls in love with him and now we're supposed to be all warm and happy like a frigging Hallmark card at Christmas time. I'm not a goddamned poster child for *Let's make lemonade out of some stupid lemons!*"

Anna took a deep breath and leaned over towards Lucas making sure she did not get too close to him physically. She did not want to cause Lucas to break off from his outpouring of vitriolic emotions. It was too important a step for him, and she was overjoyed that he was able to let it out. Some of it at any rate.

"Lucas," she whispered so softly he leaned forward to hear her, "Your father has some issues. He is human and he was very wrong with what he did to you. And he is getting the help he needs. But hating him and hating everyone around you who wants to love you will not change the facts. You know the facts. And those facts will never go away…ever. But what happened to you is in the past. And if you relive your past each and every day then you are closing the door to a beautiful future that lies in store for you.

"I need you to address what happened to you and then put it away in some place deep in your past. Perhaps then you can look at your stepfather not as a superhero but as a man who desperately wants to be a positive part of your life…That is if you will allow him in. And that includes your mother as well."

"Why?"

"Ahhh," murmured Anna, "we are all so fragile on this earth. Each day is a blessing, and I don't want you to miss out on the beauty of it all. You have a kind soul, Lucas. You have tremendous feelings that must be channeled into good if you will accept all the wonderous things that surround you. Your mother and stepfather for beginners."

"And what about my real father? Do I ever see him again? Will he always have those awful thoughts? Do I just erase him from my mind, forever?"

"Oh, Lucas. I don't think we ever erase people, good or bad, from our lives. We learn how to deal with it. We learn to open up to others and accept them. It's not easy, but Lucas, that's why I want you to keep coming here. I want to talk with you. I want to hear about what you're thinking, and feeling, and most importantly how you will be growing. You have so much to offer this world, Lucas, and I do not want to see you use hatred and anger to drive you every day. Not when there is another side to Lucas Cannon that needs to sprout out of his hardened shell and show the world what you are truly capable of becoming."

Lucas stared at Anna. He rested his hands on his chin and spoke so softly that Anna had to tilt her head to make sure she heard him. "Miss Anna, will you help me?"

CHAPTER 40

Back to school. They stood together in Dr. Libertino's office, shuffling their feet, exchanging nervous looks, and suppressing scared laughter waiting for their principal to return to her office. They had been issued passes and Scott Sheldrake and Pauline Clifton had scooped them up from their first-period classes just to make sure they all landed in the main office together.

All of them filled their principal's room like it was a major press conference: Riley, Jilly, Tommy, Lucas, Junay, Sofia, Cindy, Lane, Max, Piper, Jáquan, Shaynee, Mateo, and Whitney. They stood there not sure if they were the superhero team for the school and for Mr. DeWitt or maybe they were about to be sent home. They stood, attempting to be completely still, their heads throbbing with waking up so early after a few weeks of no alarms, no bells, no pressure of school life.

"Are we in trouble?" asked Junay as she broke the silence. "I am never, ever in trouble you know. I am going to go to college on a scholarship and I cannot afford to have anything negative on my record."

"Oh, puleeze, stop your whining," chided Riley. "What we did for Mr. DeWitt was necessary."

"Yeah," chimed in Cindy, "We had to do it. We just had to."

"I don't care," added Lucas. "I'm used to being in this office. I'm used to getting into trouble. Junay, you're such a goody-goody. Besides, Dr. L. always has cool shit on her desk. Look at that candy bowl!" Lucas took a step towards Dr. Libertino's desk where a decorated bowl of mixed miniature candies sat waiting to be grabbed.

"Lucas, dude," hissed Tommy in a scared voice, "don't touch anything. Hell, we'll get in more trouble than we must already be in."

Max mumbled something unintelligible, and Sofia nudged him with her elbow. "Huh? Waddya saying?"

"Jeez, look at her pictures, everyone. I didn't know she had a black husband!"

The group suddenly all shifted to staring at Lila's bookcase which was filled with pictures of her husband Darrius and her two children, Bessie and Benjamin.

Max took a step forward and pointed at the pictures. "See? Look at that, willya?"

Dr. Lila Libertino slipped into her office just as the group of students were gawking at her family pictures on her bookcase while Lucas Cannon's hand was wrist-deep in her candy bowl.

She smiled, the joy reaching her 'Alice Blue' eyes which

only added to those laugh lines. She cleared her throat and suddenly every student turned around as if on cue, their faces swiftly outlined in a mixture of fear, nervousness, and awkwardness.

"Good morning, group. It's a pleasure to see all of you in my office first thing this morning. I see you all received the passes I sent to your first-period classes."

There was a quietness in the room. Nobody was ready to speak. The fear was palpable and if there was a smell to it, oddly enough, they would have said it smelled like hot chocolate.

Lila laughed as her secretary Amelia slid in behind her with a huge tray of cups filled with foaming hot chocolate.

"Okay, my young lovies. Find a chair and sit down. Of course, like Lucas here, you may enjoy a treat from my candy dish to go along with the hot chocolate my wonderful secretary has prepared for you. Now turn around and say thank you, Ms. Goddard."

If this was an underwater scene you would have thought they were a group of guppies with their mouths wide open gulping for air. Immediately and in unison, the bobbleheads moved up and down and recited, "Thank you, Ms. Goddard."

Each student approached the candy dish with caution, took a few of their favorites, and found a chair. They sat down quietly and waited as Amelia walked around to each of them and carefully handed them a napkin first and then a disposable mug of steaming hot chocolate.

"Oh, God," cooed Junay. "I love hot chocolate. Oh, this is the absolute bomb, Dr. Libertino."

"Please call me Dr. L. It's easier. And you are very welcome. All of you are. And now, relax. You are not in trouble. I repeat you are not in trouble.

An audible sigh wafted across the room and fourteen pairs of shoulders seemed to sink as the cups were raised to their lips and slurping sounds filled the room.

Lila looked at the group. She stared at who she thought was Linette Hong, but her new hairstyle screamed something else. Lila realized she was staring so she quickly adjusted her gaze to the others when Linette stood up and said, "It's okay, Dr. L. It's me, Linette, but from now on would you please call me Lane?"

Lila nodded, swallowed the hot coffee a little too quickly, and had a coughing fit. "I'm sorry, Lin…..Lane…I will remember that."

Lila stood up. "Please continue enjoying your hot chocolate and the snacks that you have scooped up from my desk." Lila grinned and chuckled as the group stopped eating in mid-stream, suddenly feeling guilty. "No, no…. please continue. It's just that in a second I am going to ask Ms. Atkinson and Mr. Sheldrake to join us."

"Dr. L?" asked Max. "Are we in trouble or something? I mean I know some of us got into trouble over break…" he looked accusingly over at Riley and Lucas and continued to speak, his mouth full, "but our parents know about it and, uh, well, I guess we all had to deal with our own consequences. You know what I mean?"

Lila frowned. She immediately thought about her own two children and how she would have handled her situation had she found Benji or Bessie inebriated at their home, much less at someone else's home. Lila did not have the chance to think much longer as Barbara Atkinson and Scott Sheldrake entered her office.

Both Scott and Barbara looked around the room at the group of teenagers laughing and sucking down hot chocolate and shoving candy bars into their mouths as though they had not eaten in days.

Scott laughed as he announced, "Well, good morning again, group! What a fine team we have here this morning!"

It was harder for Barbara to be as jovial as Scott, but she added, somewhat hesitantly, "Hello, everyone. And thank you for being here."

Riley stopped chewing her Snickers candy bar and mumbled through the muck in her mouth, "So, why exactly are we here?"

Lila stood up, took a long, drawn-out breath, and very humbly said, "I called all of you in this morning, well, simply to thank you."

Max swallowed his hot chocolate and began choking on it because he swallowed it so quickly, gulped for air and asked, "Huh? Why?"

"Because," Lila continued, "Because all of you demonstrated such bravery when each of you sent me an email explaining why you so strongly believed Mr. DeWitt needed to be back in the classroom.

"At first I was worried that one of you," and she looked directly at Riley, "that one of you would write an email and that each of you would just copy, paste, and send, but no, every email was unique to the writer, and I appreciated that most of all."

The group was all in various stages of smiling, chewing, nodding their heads up and down, and high-fiving one another.

Riley felt the need, however, to stand up. She had started the whole email task force and wanted to clear up some things. "You know, Dr. L., I may not be in that special afternoon group that some of these guys are in, but I have Mr. DeWitt as a teacher, and I knew we had to do something. I knew you needed to hear from all of us and if you need more emails…"

Lila interrupted Riley, "Oh, please, no, I think we have enough. In fact, Ms. Atkinson, Mr. Sheldrake, and I will be leaving in a few minutes to speak with the assistant superintendent about your emails and a few other things."

Lucas's head suddenly shot up. "Uhhh, are we gonna get called or something? I mean, do we have to go somewhere and talk to people?"

Scott took the lead here, seeing how nervous Lucas was acting. "No, my good man, you do not have to go anywhere or speak to anyone. Your emails were more than enough.

Barbara interjected, "You see not only have you done the right thing, and I am so proud of all of you as well, but some teachers have stepped up and shared some important information with me.

There was an audible sigh from the group and more

slurping and chewing sounds lightened the tension as quickly as a morning fog gets lifted from the sun.

"As a matter of fact," added Lila, "the three of us are heading out now, but we wanted to thank you and show our appreciation for your courage and your ability to demonstrate your convictions through your emails to me.

"Now, I want you to finish your treats but do not take more than the next twenty minutes and get back to your classes. We good?"

Lots of thanks and okays and whews were shared as the three adults looked at each other while Lila grabbed her briefcase, and they exited the office.

There was a hush until Riley looked at everyone and said, "First of all, I want to apologize for what happened at my house."

Lucas jumped in, "No, Riley girl, it's me who needs to apologize. I should never have put everyone in that situation. M'bad, yo and I will never do that again."

Cindy braved a comment, "Thanks, Riley. It's because of you and your mom that I was able to get through the break. It hasn't been so easy for me."

Lane jumped in, "And hey, thank you guys for accepting me. I guess I'm going through some shi….stuff and I needed your support."

"Okay," interjected Junay, "This isn't a frigging Oprah show. I don't even know half the stuff you're talking about, but I need to get to class because I have a quiz in second period and I am not even close to being ready!"

Laughter, giggles, a few loud burps, and more high-fives as the group finished their treats, placed the cups on the tray on the table, and headed out to pick up their passes to return to class.

CHAPTER 41

Beverly sat at her desk in her classroom, her small dark eyes shining as she read her emails on her computer. Her wrist had finally healed; her bruises from Ted had faded and she was going to file divorce papers on him later that day. She felt if Ted wanted to hook up with his secretary, well, then good riddance to him and good luck to her. She can have him. I'm done.

Her phone dinged notifying her that a text message had just come through. It was from Alisa. She had not spoken to Alisa since way before the break, and there had been a growing awkward silence between them.

Beverly read the text and then reread it again. She could not believe her eyes.

> Hello, Beverly. I know we have not talked in quite some time, but I needed to let you know that I spoke with Ms. Atkinson before the school break. I told her many things that afternoon, but the most important

part of our conversation was that I truly believed you lied about Carl DeWitt. He is a good man, an outstanding teacher, and a decent human being. I could not go on living with your lies about him. I also told Cassandra because she and Carl had been dating and it was not fair that she should be in the dark all this time. She was hurting and it wasn't fair.

That's all. I guess our friendship at this point is a thing of the past. I always felt you were just angry with the world, but I never thought you would go to such lengths as to ruin a man's life because of your petty jealousy.

If we bump into each other in the halls, and that's bound to happen, well, I'll just nod but don't expect me to sit with you and carry on like we're BFFs or something.

Good luck, Beverly. I hope one day you will be able to shed some of your anger and realize that most people are truly good, hard-working individuals.

Take care, Alisa.

Beverly automatically placed her finger on the message section as though she was about to reply to Alisa's text. She thought about it some more, put her phone down on the desk, and stood up. She looked at her clock and saw that she still had a good thirty minutes until her next class.

"I'll be damned if I'm going to sit here and allow that bitch to slander me like that," Beverly muttered aloud, her lips curling up almost like a vicious dog ready to hurl an attack and her small pellet-shaped eyes darkened with hatred that thrived from deep within her withered soul.

Beverly stormed out of her classroom and marched down the hall to the main office. "I'm going to tear a new one in that Barbara Atkinson," Beverly uttered to herself. "She'll never know what that lying Alisa is unquestionably all about saying those vile things about me. How dare she get away with that? If Battle Axe wants to know the real truth about some of the teachers around here, well, she's going to get an earful."

Just as Beverly was turning the corner, what looked like a pack of unruly teenagers surged out of the main office giggling loudly as though a party had just ended. She could hear their raucous laughter as they were poking each other, shoving jokingly, and pretending to be dancing with each other.

Beverly's anger unleashed its fury. "Get out of my damn way!" she barked at Lucas and Max and Cindy as the three of them were still blocking the doorway to the office.

"Move aside now, dammit, I said! Get back to your class before I report the whole lot of you!"

Junay stared at Beverly in shock. "It's okay, Mrs. Wine-wrought. We have passes. We are not in trouble."

"I don't care what you have. You don't belong here now. Move along and stop all that laughing. Classes are in session or don't you even pay attention! Ungrateful snots!"

Riley and Jilly stared at each other in disbelief, but rather than react to Mrs. Winewrought, the two of them started snickering and pushing each other. The others joined in with comments of "oooh, I'm scared", "hurry up, we are such bad children" and "oh, I'm gonna have detention for sure this time!"

Beverly's fury had bubbled over beyond her ability to control herself, but she knew instinctively this was not going to go over well, so she pushed her way through the young crowd, yanked open the door, and almost fell as she tripped over her feet in the main office.

Cassandra looked up suddenly to see Mrs. Winewrought in such obvious distress. She stood up at her desk and said as softly and calmly as she could, "Mrs. Winewrought, are you okay? Can I help you? Do you need something?"

"Don't you come near me, you little slut! I know you have been sneaking out with that lowlife Carl DeWitt. I know you've been talking about me. I know you are telling lies about me. Don't think I don't know what you truly are – a two-bit secretary who is looking for a husband and any guy will do.

"Now tell me right now where is BA…I mean Ms. Atkinson? I need to see her immediately if not sooner. I know where her office is and I'm just going there right now."

Cassandra jumped away from her desk both in shock and dismay at seeing Beverly Winewrought losing control. She stepped in front of Beverly hoping to calm her down.

"It's alright, Mrs. Winewrought," whispered Cassandra so as not to draw any more attention to the situation. There were a few parents in the waiting area and the other two secretaries had already poked their heads out of their doors.

"Get out of my way, Ms. Conway. I'm going to see Atkinson like I said."

"But…b..b…but…Mrs. Winewrought," Cassandra pleaded.

Amelia Goddard, Lila's secretary suddenly appeared from her office and swiftly glided over and blocked Beverly from progressing any closer towards the assistant principals' offices. "Mrs. Winewrought I overheard you needed to see Ms. Atkinson. Well, Ms. Atkinson is not in the building right now. How can I be of help?"

Beverly stood still. This complicated things. This was not her plan. She wanted to barge into Atkinson's office and demand an apology.

"Well," argued Beverly, "Then I will see Dr. Libertino. It's an emergency."

Beverly sidestepped past Amelia but Joanne Cumberly, Barbara Atkinson's secretary, came to the rescue. "Why, hello, Mrs. Winewrought. How can I be of assistance today?"

Beverly reached out her arms to push Joanne but pulled herself back, realizing she was about to go too far. She heard some other noises and realized a few teachers were suddenly stepping out of the teachers' mail room aware and concerned with hearing the ruckus.

"Where are the administrators? Why aren't they here in the building? It's a

regular school day. Who's running this asylum? The secretaries? I demand to know what's happening here?"

The three secretaries huddled together whispering while Amelia was also speaking into her walkie. In a matter of seconds security Pauline Clifton burst through the door and quickly analyzing the situation turned to Amelia Goddard and spoke rapidly to her, "Ms. Goddard, walkie Nurse Kelly and tell her to get over here. STAT!"

Pauline saw Beverly attempting to bulldoze her way down the hall and she rushed over to join her. "Hey, Mrs. Winewrought, how are you doing today, huh?"

Beverly turned, her eyes glazed with rage, and with great annoyance looked at Pauline and said as snidely as she could, "Go away from me before I spit on you like I did your boss!"

Pauline recognized a woman out of control having worked in the penitentiary system, and knew she was capable of doing great harm so she positioned herself at a 45-degree angle from her and continued to follow her.

"Move away….now…" Beverly whistled angrily through her teeth.

Pauline ignored her and stayed with her as she shoved Lila's door open, saw that it was empty, and slammed it shut. Then she raced to Barbara Atkinson's door and thrust it open only to realize it too was empty. She yanked it so hard that there was a sound of broken glass that must have been shaken and crashed to the floor. Beverly spun around to see Pauline right on her side. Her eyes were wild with fury and she was losing her self-control. "Go away from me. I mean it."

Pauline nodded, but there was no way she would leave her side. She knew when someone was in such distress that their mind and their body were no longer in control of their actions. She followed Beverly as she made her way down the hall and stopped in front of Jeff Stineman's office.

The door was closed, but this did not stop Beverly. She did not knock; instead, she heaved the heavy door open and found Jeff with his back to her as he was quietly speaking with someone on his cell phone.

Beverly pounced into the room and before she could slam his door closed, Pauline had slid in behind her and she was not about to leave. She knew that Nurse Kelly would be here any moment and she needed the doorway accessible.

Jeff turned around, incredulous at what he was seeing before him. There was PC as she was affectionately called, with one hand keeping his door ajar, and Beverly Winewrought, standing right in front of him with her eyes ablaze, spittle dribbling down her chin and both her hands clenched in tight fists.

Jeff put his cell phone down on his desk and spoke slowly and calmly, "Good morning, Mrs. Winewrought. Is there something I can help you with this morning?"

Beverly could not see straight. Things were becoming

blurry in her mind, her vision playing tricks on her as well, but she spat out, "Don't you fucking placate me, you low life for an administrator. I need to let you know that one of your teachers has lied about me and I will not tolerate it. I will not stand for it! I want action and I want it now!"

As she spoke, her voice got louder and shriller and her arms flailed as she got closer to Jeff's desk. She was no longer in control of her voice, her words, or her arms. Her arms started swinging to and fro, her white lab coat had come undone, and an earring flew off onto Jeff's desk. She saw her gold hoop spiraling onto his desk and as she lurched forward to grab it her loose lab coat caught on Jeff's purple glass vase that held his artificial bouquet of dried flowers.

As though it were happening in slow motion, Nurse Kelly emerged from out of nowhere, Pauline lunged forward and then swayed sideways to try to catch the vase, Amelia, who had steered Nurse Kelly into the room was now suddenly behind Beverly grabbing her firmly by her shoulders, Jeff was standing up, his mouth wide open and the vase bounced off the table and flew into the windowsill crashing into a thousand pieces of shattered purple prisms that turned the room into a moving purple kaleidoscope.

Beverly's mind went blank. She was nineteen years old, and she had come home late from a party. Her father was waiting for her bellowing at her that he had already called the police. She was so nervous that she accidentally knocked over the family vase in the living room when she tried to run to her bedroom. It shattered into a million multicolored pieces on the floor and when she looked up her father was standing over her swinging his baseball bat towards her head.

But Beverly, staring at Jeff Stineman, did not see Jeff; she saw her father and he was going to beat her. Beverly screamed, slowly at first and then faster and faster, and then the words poured out of her, "He saw my vajayjay! Oh, my God, Daddy, he saw my vajayjay. Stop him from seeing it, Daddy. Stop him, now. Oh, God, please, help me from him seeing it. Don't hurt me, Daddy, don't hurt me, Daddy, oh, God, please help me!"

Beverly crumpled in a heap onto the floor as Amelia, still holding onto her shoulders, guided her gently down. Nurse Kelly rushed over to her and with help from Pauline, they gently laid her on her side as the tears poured down her face and she sobbed uncontrollably.

The EMTs had been called the minute the other secretaries heard the screaming and now as the medical team entered the main office, they ushered everyone out of the area so they could have some privacy.

They found a woman curled up in a fetal position on the floor in one of the administrator's offices with female security, a secretary, and the school nurse on the floor gently massaging the woman's back, saying soothing words to her that no one else could hear.

The two EMTs carefully lifted the woman onto a gurney and swiftly rolled her out to the waiting ambulance and within minutes the ambulance had left the parking lot.

It took only fifteen minutes for the entire frightening

scene to have passed and then the main office was back in order with everyone at their desks as if nothing had just occurred, but behind the doors of Jeff Stineman's office, Nurse Kelly, Pauline Clifton and Jeff sat in disbelief at what had just transpired as though they had just witnessed a horror film written by Stephen King.

Quietly, a retired gray-haired elderly teacher wearing an old lab coat and a pair of bifocals stuck on his forehead, entered the main office. He smiled at Cassandra because he knew her well, having taught at the school for so many years.

"Why, hello, Ms. Conway. How are you doing today? You called me in to sub?"

CHAPTER 42

Carl sat in the central office waiting room with Lemont Jacobs, his union representative. Lemont, with his large, coffee-colored almond-shaped eyes glanced at Carl. There were deep worry lines etched on Carl's forehead and Lemont immediately felt his pain.

Lemont whispered to Carl, "It's cool, man. We got this covered. This is going to be over today. You hear me? By the way, do you have copies of those emails I forwarded to you and asked you to bring for today's hearing?"

Carl reached into his briefcase and pulled out a handful of printed emails. Everyone he had asked to write to him had quickly responded to both him and Lemont, no questions asked. He closed his briefcase and placed it on the chair next to him, casually resting his hand on the soft leather of the case. It was a gift from his father the day he earned his teaching degree.

He looked at Lemont, his brown eyes watering. "I can't believe the things that my colleagues wrote about me." And then he thought to himself, *Oh, God, especially Cassandra.*

She was so sweet and her words....oh, please, let me be able to see her again. I think I fell in love with her on that first day when she smiled at me. Don't let this be the last time...

And then Carl's voice cracked. He could not hold back the tears. "They were so warm and positive and generous. I never knew. I never knew how well-liked I was at school.

"I don't know what to say, Lemont. I don't know what to say to the panel in that room. I didn't do what they accused me of doing. I'm still not even sure what the hell they are saying I did. And I'll be damned if I still don't know who even fucking accused me, but, Lemont, I swear to God on the bible, I didn't do anything inappropriate. I didn't do anything wrong. I'm a good guy and I'm a good teacher."

Lemont observed Carl and arrived at the same conclusion he had felt the day he met this gentle soul of a teacher.

Lemont spoke gently to Carl, "Man, I've worked with a lot of people in my field where I know in my gut that a person is as guilty as sin as soon as I say hello, but I can tell you…. I can tell you, Carl, I believe you. I believe every word you have said to me since I contacted you. I see it in your eyes; I feel it in your heart. I know you're a good guy, Carl, and I just hope that everyone we talk to today will see it, too. I need you to listen to me, now. Really, really listen to me before we go in there. You know the truth. You know exactly who you are and what kind of human being you have always been – in and out of that classroom. You speak your truth, man. And you just be cool. I want you to look everyone in the eye! I repeat… always… always look them in the eye and don't stop. It's okay if you're crying here; it's okay. I just want you to talk to that panel with all of your heart. I know you to be real. Let them see all these letters that your colleagues wrote. Let them see you and know your truth and your passion for teaching and learning.

"Carl, at the end of the meeting, I believe with all my heart and all my experience that this group of educators…. this group, well, they'll know…. they'll know God's honest truth."

The door opened from the conference room. Carl's head snapped up and he quickly wiped his nose with his sleeve.

Exiting the room were Dr. Lila Libertino, Barbara Atkinson, Scott Sheldrake, and Alisa Saper.

Carl immediately stood up. As soon as he saw Alisa, Carl's face scrunched up in a tight ball of wrinkles and lines. He looked at her quizzically.

"Alisa? What? Huh? Why? Did I do something to you? Did I hurt you? Offend you? God, please tell me."

Barbara Atkinson quickly grabbed Alisa by the arm and looped her own arm through Alisa. Barbara looked at Carl and with deep respect in her voice calmly stated, "No, Carl. Alisa did not say anything to implicate you. In fact, Carl, it was Alisa who came forward to tell me that you had been wronged. Someone in the building had been spreading lies and…."

Alisa interrupted Barbara. "Thank you, Ms. Atkinson, but I do want to tell Carl." She stepped away from Barbara and Lila. She took Carl's hands in hers and with her soft amber eyes she whispered, "Carl, first of all, you need to know that I have always believed in you. I am only so very sorry that I did not come to seek you out right away. That was wrong of me, and I apologize from the bottom of my heart. I was scared. I was selfish to hold back that information and it took someone very special in my life to make me see that I needed to speak the truth."

Carl stood there, looking at Alisa's eyes that were overflowing with tears. They were still holding hands as Barbara and Lila, Scott and even Lemont kept their distance. This needed to happen and sadly it should have happened months ago and then Carl would not have suffered so much.

Carl felt the room spinning and his eyes saw stars floating above him. Scott observed this and rushed over to grab Carl before he fell to the floor. He wrapped his arms around Carl's shoulders, pulled him carefully away from Alisa and guided him to the chair behind him.

Carl blanked out and did not remember Scott coming to his rescue but as he slowly opened his eyes, the room stopped spinning and Scott Sheldrake was sitting next to him with a bottle of water.

"Here, Carl," he murmured softly. "Take a sip, man. You're okay, but we kinda lost you there for a minute. Take some slow, deep breaths, a sip of the water, and give yourself a few minutes."

Carl looked around to see the same faces staring at him with a mixture of compassion and pity and love. He didn't feel comfortable, as a matter of fact, he felt incredibly embarrassed by the entire episode.

He took a few gulps of the water bottle and passed it back to Scott.

"I am so confused over everything that is happening."

Carl looked at Alisa who was openly crying; she could not hold back her emotions. Then he gazed at Barbara Atkinson and then at his principal, Lila.

Lila stepped forward. "Mr. DeWitt, Carl, let me speak for the group so I can clear up any misunderstandings. You are about to go into the conference room that we just left. While we were in there, Ms. Saper here explained that she was privy to some texts from one of your colleagues, Beverly Winewrought, who openly admitted to Alisa that she had been lying about any inappropriate behaviors she claimed you committed.

"Ms. Saper approached Ms. Atkinson with this knowledge right before the winter break and shared this information with me. Mr. Jacobs, your representative, notified me that we would have this hearing today and did we want to present any pertinent information. Well, along with Ms. Saper's statement, it seems that you have quite a following of students at our school. They took the time over break to email me personally with incredible stories of your kindness, your compassion, and your unbelievable encouragement that you provide them with on a daily basis. And, I shared all of these emails with the panel this morning."

Carl sat there stunned. He was overcome with emotions, but he wasn't sure as to what to say next. He stared at the group; his mouth wide open but no words could emerge.

Lila continued, "And now, Mr. DeWitt, it's your turn to go into that conference room and demonstrate to the panel what we have always known – that you are an exceptional teacher at Wells, and we cannot wait to have you rejoin us!"

At that exact moment, the door to the conference room opened and a woman wearing a black and white pin-striped suit looked out into the waiting room and seeing Lemont, motioned for him to enter and to bring his client with him.

That was the signal for the group to leave and return to school. Carl's throat was tight, but he managed to squeak, his voice cracking through the words, "Thank you, everyone. Thank you from the bottom of my heart." Lemont nodded to everyone, and with his hand on Carl's back moved to enter the conference room.

• • •

Carl's hands were ice cold as he sat in the large conference room with Lemont facing four adults whom he knew by face and name but had never encountered close up. He was intimidated, frightened, and angry which, when mixed together, gave him enough courage to sit up straight and look at each one of the high-powered individuals in their eyes.

Carl knew that depending on what he said, how he said it, and if they believed him, he would either have his job back or he would have to walk out of there and find a new career.

"Let's begin this meeting," declared Dr. Belluah Stanson.

"Good morning, Mr. Jacobs and Mr. DeWitt. With me today are the following directors: Dr. Stanley Morefeld, Dr. Constance Hyde, and Dr. Isawald Littleton."

Each director nodded as Dr. Stanson introduced them and Carl nodded back in recognition. Carl felt as though he should have stood up, maybe shaken their hands, but Lemont kept his hand pressed down on Carl's forearm with a tacit understanding not to move.

"As you know, Mr. DeWitt, you have been suspended from teaching due to an allegation of inappropriate behaviors with students. I am sure you can understand that we take these matters seriously and because of that we had to suspend you in order to conduct a complete and thorough investigation of the matter."

Carl clasped his hands together tightly to keep the panel from noticing how much they were shaking. His knee was doing gymnastics under the table and Lemont gently put his hand on Carl's knee to stop it from shaking up and down.

Dr. Stanson, removing her reading glasses from her long nose, continued, "This morning I heard from one of your colleagues that the allegation was based on untruths and that this colleague was suffering from some personal issues that may have caused her to believe in her own vicious tales. Whether it was bred from jealousy, hatred, or some other deeper neurosis this individual will be receiving the mental health help she needs.

"However, Mr. DeWitt, I know that this proceeding includes your side of the situation, and my panel is anxiously awaiting to hear your statement. But before you begin, we would like to offer you our deepest sympathies on the loss of your mother."

Dr. Stanson took a moment to allow Carl to gather himself as she could see that his red and swollen eyes were telling her so much of his character without him ever saying a word.

"So, Mr. DeWitt, would you please now share with us anything you want us to hear?"

Carl took a soul-searching deep breath, wiped his eyes with the back of his hand, and stood up. He looked at each one sitting there knowing that they were judging him, and he felt insecure for a moment, but then he thought back to the past months when he was so hurt and depressed to the point he was even considering taking his own life. And then he shook his head, shaking out the doubt and the anger and mistrust that had been laid upon him and he knew this was his moment in time and he would not let it pass him without shouting to the world, well, these four individuals, about his innocence.

And so he began, slowly at first and then with more urgency and volume and passion.

"Thank you for seeing me today. And thank you for your condolences. My mother was a very important part of my life. She was a positive influence. She taught me humility, and a pride in all that I do, and along with that she gave me a wonderful sense of humor and a deep compassion for everyone I meet.

"I love what I do. I wake up every morning with a smile

knowing that each day I get to enrich my students' lives not just with the textbook knowledge I share, but with a zest for life and learning. There is no judgment in my classroom. There is no room for sarcasm or belittling or making one feel small. I know what that feels like, and I refuse to ever let a student of mine feel that pain."

The panel was completely engrossed in Carl's statement. They nodded their heads, and they smiled, not big open-mouth smiles, but tiny, I-believe-in-you smiles.

Carl continued. "When Ms. Atkinson asked me to work with a mentoring group, I was shocked; I was in disbelief. I know I have not been teaching for very long, but this was a lifelong dream of mine – to work with students who need that extra ounce of confidence and belief in who they are and to know they can achieve. I knew that I was going to work with an extremely gifted and talented teacher, Mrs. Waverly, so I never doubted what we could build together.

"And things were going great; at least I thought they were until that one day when I was escorted out of the building. I was shocked, scared, and hurt. I did not know who to turn to."

Carl turned to look at Lemont. "And Mr. Jacobs, here, well, he has been my rock. When I thought all was lost, Mr. Jacobs believed in me. He kept my spirits up; he kept me going. Thank you, Lemont. I owe you my life." Lemont smiled and nodded. Carl did not want the attention on Lemont too long, so he quickly looked up at the panel.

"I have shared with you letters that my colleagues have written about me, and I hope you can see it in your hearts to know that I did not ever do anything inappropriate to anyone, ever – in my life. I love my teaching position…" Carl choked up for a minute. He looked down, then he looked up at the ceiling as though he were looking at his mother and at Emma. Then he smiled, knowingly.

"Thank you for listening to me today. I wish you all a great day."

And Carl sat down. Lemont handed him a tissue and Carl blew his nose.

Dr. Stanson cleared her throat, looked at her colleagues, and stood up.

"Mr. DeWitt, I want to thank you for sharing with us today. We have read your letters from your colleagues along with numerous letters from your students."

Carl's eyes widened and his mouth opened when he heard that. He did not know his students had written letters.

"Mr. Jacobs, we want to thank you for all the hard work you have done with this investigation. You have completed a job well done, sir.

"And so, Mr. DeWitt I am so sorry you have had to endure this as long as you have. I applaud your profession-alism and strength in these investigations. And so it is the total agreement of this panel, along with your principal, that we are to reinstate you to your position effective im-mediately. We are done today. That is all."

Carl stood up, laughed and cried and shouted without realizing he had just burst out in triumph. He turned to Lemont and gave him a huge bear hug.

"Thank you, Lemont. Oh, dear God, thank you! Can we leave now?"

Lemont smiled, and exclaimed, "Oh, yeah! We are so done!!"

Carl turned to the panel and cried, "Thank you, everyone!"

He turned and left the room, but his feet never touched the floor.

CHAPTER 43

Carl was just a little bit hesitant when he was about to enter the building. It had been so long and the last time he was inside, he was being accompanied to his car under very guarded explanations by a police officer.

He arrived early thinking he could slip into his classroom without anyone noticing. He was so wrong! He opened his door gently and was blown away by what he saw. Students were holding up signs decorated with colorful lettering that said WELCOME BACK and WE MISSED YOU and WE LOVE YOU, MR. DEWITT.

The room was a wall-to-wall mass of bodies from his students to teachers and even some parents he recognized. Scott Sheldrake was in the front of the room smiling from ear to ear and standing next to him was Neva Waverly who was crying unapologetically.

His desk was covered with confetti and topped with cupcakes and juice boxes and individual candies strewn all around.

The shouting and the cheering as Carl entered the room could be heard all the way down the hall. Shouts of "DE-WITT…DEWITT….DEWITT!" were screamed over and over and over again.

Carl was overwhelmed with joy, shock, awe, and honor. He put his briefcase next to his desk and he turned to face the crowd. He was never one who felt comfortable in front of a crowd; teaching his class of students was one thing, but this, well, he was so overcome with emotion that he just stood there and smiled. The room exploded with clapping and cheers and shouts of glee.

Finally, Carl put his arms up in the air and quieted the room

"I…I…don't know what to say," he stammered. "I am so incredibly happy to be here with you. I am so thankful to each and every one of you and I am grateful and … wait…more than that…I am so honored to be called your teacher."

The room burst into cheering again and this time Carl stood up on a chair and quieted the group again.

"I see some of you went to the trouble to supply us with a hearty breakfast here," he quipped. Laughter and chuckles raced around the room like the wind over the fields. "I don't know how to do this in any kind of orderly fashion," he laughed and turned to Scott and Neva, "but if my friends here will help me, I am sure every one of you will get a treat this morning.

"I want you to know," Carl choked on his words, "I want you all to know how much I have missed you, how much I wanted to be with you, and how eternally indebted I am to all of you for supporting me. I'm back. I'm back for good and I will be your teacher today and for always! So, thank you, and let's get a food line going here!"

The day flew by and Carl was overjoyed with each class. He knew that tomorrow he would get back into the actual curriculum he was teaching, but the love he felt today carried him and he floated with each passing class time.

At the end of the day, Neva came over to see how he was doing and to remind him that they still had to teach their after-school mentoring class.

"Oh, my goodness, Neva," Carl spilled his cupcake crumbs in his hand as he spoke. "Neva, I'm not prepared; I did not plan anything with you. Oh, I am so sorry, and I feel foolish to just sit there."

Neva grinned. "Don't be silly, my boy. I've got it all planned. The lesson today will be joyful. It will be tearful. And it will show you how much your kids missed you. Oh, and I am inviting Riley Maddox to join us today. She isn't really in the group, but she has been totally instrumental in helping guide or should I say, motivate, cajole, inspire….uh, demand that your students send emails to Dr. Libertino over the break. And, boy, did they ever. She's quite a leader and I know how much she adores you and quite frankly, they all do."

Carl was nonplussed. He did not know what to say, and fortunately, he did not have time to compose anything as the group began pouring in almost immediately after school was dismissed.

The students automatically turned the classroom into their circle of desks. Their bookbags were strewn around the room, coats and sweatshirts thrown on top of the bags, cell phones were turned off and then there they sat, waiting with the same intensity of a Christmas morning.

Neva broke the ice. "Good afternoon, everyone. Thank you for being on time. You are my magnificent dozen except today we are truly a baker's dozen. Please welcome Riley Maddox, who you all know. She will be a part of our group today."

Soft sounds were welcoming Riley, including Lucas who just snorted and spouted out, "Hey Maddog."

Neva continued. "We have been working very hard all semester, and today before we get involved in our second semester's agenda, I hoped that we could take this opportunity to go around the room and let Mr. DeWitt know how much you have grown from being together. What you have learned about yourself, about others, and how that has made a difference in your life. Well, at least I hope so. And therefore, without further ado, let's begin. In no special order, we can just go around the circle."

Tommy started, "I'm gonna go first so I don't have to think about it any longer. This group has been – like cool. I don't think I would have done as well this semester without you guys and, like, Mr. DeWitt, man if it wasn't for you… and Mrs. Waverly, too, I think I would have stayed home most days. So thanks for, well, you know, everything."

Max jumped in next. "Okay, Tommy, you're cool, man. I gotta say, though, this group, well," and Max looked at

Sofia who turned several shades of red from her neck up to her hairline, "I met my Sofia girl and she is everything to me. But for real, I know I can do so much more than I realized and it's all because when I come here after school, I know I'm in a safe place and nobody is gonna laugh at me no matter how dumb I can sound sometimes. So, like, thanks."

"Safe," Cindy began, "That's such a little word but it can mean everything. I know I have anxieties but when I'm here, like Max, I feel safe and I know that anything I say, you know, you're not going to laugh at me." Cindy looked over at Riley and added, "My mom has cancer. Wow, that's the first time I have said that out loud because saying it means it's for real and, yeah, she could die from it." Cindy took a deep breath.

"She has breast cancer. Actually, it is called triple-negative breast cancer and it's because of Riley that I'm even functioning. You see, Riley and her whole family took me in while my mom was going through treatments. My mom had a friend stay with her, but she didn't want me having to be up in the middle of the night while she was throwing up or whatever she was doing. Instead, Dr. Maddox has been like a second mom to me and she helped me when I had to buy my mom a wig and some new clothes because she's been losing so much weight," Cindy tried to hold back tears but they spilled over sluicing down her cheeks as she pushed her glasses up tight, "I don't know what I would have done without Riley's family right now. I'm so grateful for them…and for all of you."

Everyone looked over at Riley and started clapping. Riley, who never feels embarrassed at anything, started fidgeting and clasping her hands together. Finally, she spoke, "Look, it's okay. Cindy can be a real pain in the ass if you know what I mean." Riley looked around the room as everyone smiled and laughed, but not in a malicious way, no, it was more like laughing at your sibling. "But," Riley continued, "I don't have a sister, so it was kinda cool to have her around. And Cindy cannot in any way shape or form cook to save her soul, so I have a lot of work to do!" Again, the group snickered and made some other noises as they remembered eating the huge breakfast at Riley's house before they all started drinking. "Anyway, thanks for letting me sit in today. I think this is a cool group to hang out with, that is except for Lucas!"

Lucas's head shot up! He wasn't going to add anything today, but hearing his name called out, he exclaimed, "Listen, Maddog, you are one helluva cook, but your after-eating parties suck, man!" Everyone in the circle nodded their heads remembering how awful they felt after drinking the liquor that Lucas had brought, but more importantly, they remembered having to call their parents to come pick them up and the consequences each of them had once they returned home.

"But, Mr. DeWitt," Lucas added, "I know I don't always show up here all the time, and Mrs. Waverly is forever going after me..." Lucas stopped and stared at Mrs. Waverly who smiled knowingly and nodded in a motherly fashion. "But when I do come here, I always feel better

when I leave. I'm glad you're back. I missed you. And…
well…okay then, I'm done. Thanks."

Carl nodded and then without meaning to, stared at
Lane. He looked confused but Lane quickly helped him
out, "It's okay, Mr. DeWitt. I cut my hair and I am wearing
some different clothes and if it's okay with you I'd like you
to call me Lane from now on."

Carl smiled. "I think you are very brave and courageous,
Lane, and I applaud your strength. If you ever feel overwhelmed with anything regarding your identity, please
come see me. I never want you to feel alone as you continue
to grow and shape your future."

And so, each student shared their appreciation for the
group, Mrs. Waverly, and for Carl's return. The afternoon
session flew by quickly and before they knew it the time
to end the class had approached.

The students got up slowly, almost reluctantly, and re-
arranged the desks and chairs back to their original places,
grabbed their coats, and slung the bookbags over their
shoulders. They seemed to be in no particular hurry to
leave as Carl and Neva stood at the door saying their personal goodbyes. A few of the students stopped and hugged
Carl.

After the last student had loitered long enough and
finally plodded his way out of the classroom, Carl turned
to Neva and said, "I feel like I've been reborn in some way."

Neva grinned. "Carl, what happened to you should
never have been allowed to happen. It was an awful mistake

based on a lie born out of misplaced jealousy and an un-justified revenge."

"I didn't see Beverly today," replied Carl hesitantly. "I was a bit nervous about running into her because I wasn't sure what I would say."

"You don't have to worry about that, Carl. Beverly has been admitted to a facility. She will not be returning for a while. She has had some serious issues and I think it all came to an explosive meltdown. She had to be taken away in an ambulance."

"Well, I never want to see anyone harmed, and I'm not happy that she has some mental health issues. I know what's that like as it definitely was part of my life with my sister Emma. I guess I want the best for her."

"That's very magnanimous of you, Carl, considering what you had to suffer through these past months. And no amount of 'I'm sorry' is going erase your suffering."

"No, but I feel sorry for her in a way. I would never want that burden placed on me – that is being the one to have caused another human so much heartache and misery."

The two teachers exited the classroom and anyone ob-serving them would never know the secrets they shared between them, creating a bond of friendship that would never dissolve.

Carl looked up at the ceiling in the hall. "Did they change the lights? It seems so much brighter in the hall than before."

Neva nodded. "Yes, Dr. Libertino added cameras in

all the doorways that did not have them already and demanded that the county upgrade the quality of the lights in the halls. She felt it created a more positive and healthier atmosphere where no one could hide.

"Uhhhh, Neva, would you mind if I excuse myself? I.....I....I want to see if Cassandra is still in the main office."

Neva smiled, her eyes twinkling with happiness for Carl. "Yes, you go, tiger. Go get some happiness and put some of that joy in a bottle for me!"

"Hahaha, yes, ma'am."

The two parted and Carl rushed down to the main office praying silently that Cassandra was still working.

He pushed open the office doors and there she was sitting, her long auburn hair swaying in a ponytail. She looked up to see Carl hurling himself through the door and almost falling on top of her desk.

"Hi! I mean, hello, Cassandra. God, you are beautiful. I, uh, I, well, how are you? I know I haven't been able to talk with you in a long time and I really, really missed you. Jeez, I sound like a dumb teenager on a first date and..."

Cassandra laughed nervously. She had been waiting all day for Carl to come by, praying that he would. She had heard so many different stories from every teacher who walked by her desk that day. The gossip ranged from Carl being a mass murderer to taking a hiatus in the mountains of South America somewhere to taking a job on Broadway.

"Hi, Carl. It's really good to see you again. I've missed you, too."

"So, listen, uhhhh, I'm not sure what you've heard or if you heard anything at all, but I'm super starved and I was hoping that maybe you and I…."

"Yes!" she jumped up from her desk enthusiastically. "I was just about to leave, and I am so incredibly hungry myself!"

"Perfect!" said Carl relieved. He was so nervous and now the excitement of the day, the emotions and finally seeing Cassandra.

Carl helped Cassandra put on her coat and then linked his arm through hers. "I have so much to tell you, CC. I love calling you CC. And I want you to know I have thought about you every single day. Hey, do you like Italian? Or Chinese? Or how about the new Korean Barbecue that just opened up? I hear it's the bomb!"

Arm in arm, laughing, their heads leaning into each other's, the two left the building…together.

ACKNOWLEDGEMENTS

Ilene Tockman – thank you for reading my book chapter by chapter until I was done. You always keep me focused and I love you for that! You are a treasure!

Robin Wilpon – thank you for reading and checking for my mistakes! You always seem to find some!

Mark Rose – It's not easy when I have to keep telling you I'm busy writing when you want to do other things, but then again you knew that if I was breathing I was writing. Thank you for always understanding and being my biggest champion.

Maria A. – you are always in my thoughts and I know you are helping me from heaven.